The Secret Games of Words

STORIES

by Karen Stefano

D1522194

1 GLIMPSE
PRESS

Praise for Karen Stefano's *The Secret Games of Words*:

In *The Secret Games of Words*, Karen Stefano's intelligent debut collection of stories, time is a slippery beast. Her characters, haunted by the photo albums of their minds, straddle the chasm of past and present with equal parts long-ing and bittersweet - if not bitter - nostalgia. With accomplished grace and a searing eye for detail, Stefano moves between a 1970s Southern California of puka shell necklaces, feathered hair, and Kraft mac & cheese and a wealthier modern-day landscape, where a barren backyard becomes emblematic of a ruined marriage. Peppered with absent mothers, dying fathers, angry adoles-cents, philandering husbands, and lawyers on the brink, these well-styled sto-ries emerge from the page as if "whispered by an insomniac wind." Stefano's heart is loud, and it is this steady stirring, through restless, blue-collared pasts and bleak presents, this unflagging compassion that beats through her prose, infusing her collection with depth and emotion at every turn, and allowing the reader to hope for an uncharted future.

—Sara Lippmann, author of *Doll Palace*

Reading Karen Stefano's fiction is like poring over old photographs from your childhood. There's a sense of nostalgia, that feeling of "I did that too," or "I remember that," but also a darker underlying current of loss and pain. In this collection she examines the complicated nature of relationships, familial and sexual, as well as the deep flaws within our nature—the cruelty of children, the deception of adults. It's wistful yet wise, and highly recommended.

—Pat Pujolas, author of *Jimmy Lagowski Saves the World*

Karen Stefano's debut collection, *The Secret Games of Words*, is a phenomenon. Stefano digs in and digs deep with masterful insight, piercing through the layers that separate us from the rest of humanity. Her characters store them-selves inside our cells. These stories are the landscape of us.

—Meg Tuite, author of *Bound By Blue*

Brimming with lush details and unexpected turns, every story in this collection is a marvel that transports the reader in subtle yet uncanny ways. There's something for everyone in this book, and that something might be a lit stick of dynamite, a lover gone astray, or a world sorely in need of mending. Delightful and demanding, these are stories that must be read.

—Len Kuntz, author of *The Dark Sunshine*

This is the kind of book that shoots you out of a cannon. Karen Stefano is a writer of wit, grace and guts.

—Bud Smith, author of *F-250*

Formidable, poignant and beautifully wrought, Karen Stefano slays the normal day-to-day maneuvers in her first collection of short stories. Like the title suggests, this masterpiece is filled with dark regrets, secrets, the shadows in unspeakable canyons that lie between lovers, spouses, and siblings. They sing of the real in all its glory and ugliness. Stefano's unflinching prose will leave you stunned by our human frailty.

—Robert Vaughan, author of *Addicts & Basements*

The Secret Games
of Words

STORIES

by Karen Stefano

1 GLIMPSE
PRESS

ISBN: 150254413X
ISBN 13: 9781502544131
Library of Congress Control Number: 2014917513
CreateSpace Independent Publishing Platform
North Charleston, South Carolina

ACKNOWLEDGMENTS

Thank you to the editors of the publications listed below for first publishing the following stories: "Different But The Same," *The South Carolina Review*; "Five," *The Tampa Review*; "Visitor," *Perceptions*; "How To Read Your Father's Obituary," *Santa Fe Literary Review*; "Contradiction," *Green Mountains Review*; "Telling Time," *Blue Fifth Review*; "Swoon," *Lost In Thought*; "Mystery Date," *Gloom Cupboard*; "The Rule Against Perpetuities," *Ellipsis*; "Undone," *Epiphany*. "The Secret Games of Words" and "All The Bad Words Start With V" were originally published by *Connotation Press* and "Seeing" was first published by *Metazen* and subsequently nominated for the XXXVIII Pushcart Prize.

Special thanks to the incredible Meg Tuite, Len Kuntz, and Robert Vaughan, each of whom should probably receive some kind of editor credit on this book, seeing how their brilliant minds helped shape so many of these stories. You guys are terrific writers and the best damn friends ever. Never forget our pact, okay?

Thank you to the gang at HuHaStew, particularly Kirk Hulett, Blake Harper, Dennis Stewart, Katie Gonzalez and Anita Villanueva. An all around great team and truly wonderful human beings.

Thanks to Amy Wallen, my first writing teacher, a helluva nice person whose sage advice led to publication of my first story.

Thanks to those of you who have been there for me. I love you and think you are total badasses: John Bentivoglio, Joe "take a deep breath" Bratsky, Jena Waid, Jeff Floodberg, Darlanne Mulmat, Mary Jo Boring, Ken Robidoux, Gregg Temkin, Pat Pujolas, Carole Firstman, Christopher Allen,

Dede Dulaine, Serena Suarez, Katy Radsan, Sara Lippmann, Bud Smith, Natalie Eaton, Kathy Hearn, Melissa Chadburn, Greg Vega, and Bobby Stefano. Finally, most importantly, I want to thank Janice Deaton, my BFF. JD, you are at the top of my gratitude list every single day.

For Mom & Dad

CONTENTS

THE SECRET GAMES OF WORDS

To: JackLabRat@gmail.com
Fr: missusjack1@gmail.com
Attachment: None

Dear Jack,

You've bravely opened countless Word documents of mine in recent months, yet now inexplicably refuse me any form of attachment. You know I'm not the type of woman to pass a virus. I believe in both safe sex and safe text, so it seems unfair to deny me the intimacy of an actual letter, perhaps even paranoid to reduce me to the coldness of a stand-alone email, equating me in a sense to a stranger. In any event, I ask that you *not* reply with that galling red text where you interject words between mine, launching the electronic equivalent of a screaming match where two people shout over one another, drowning each other out so that no one gets heard. In fact I ask that you not reply at all, as I hope these can be my final words to you. While we've always told some version of the truth, I'm sick of living in a truth with versions. My hope is that by reaching a bit further toward honesty I might clarify some things still rattling inside my own haggard mind.

I've been thinking about when we met at that awful party back at Berkeley —what, twenty-five years ago? We danced to The Sex Pistols, searching the rabid rhythms for permission to press against each other in the sweaty darkness. I lied that night when I said I was a virgin. I was just awkward in bed. Sex had always been messy and dull, me self-conscious, working my way through love making like I worked my way through life, making up for lack of talent with a positive attitude and lots of hard work.

But you taught me things and soon all we wanted was each other, to hear each other's stories, fresh and new as our smooth young bodies. We stayed in bed for days, wanting to confess everything, remember? I told you about my father, how he cooked dinner every night after work at the post office, asking about my day and studying instructions on a box of Kraft macaroni & cheese like it was the Rosetta Stone, how it never dawned on me until junior high that other kids had a father and a mother.

"He gave you a simple life," you said, stroking my hair.

I wanted you to make it even simpler. I whispered how you made me want to be Amish, backwards and slow, the wings of a bonnet flapping at my face and blinding me to advances of a modern world. Instead, you taught me the Playboy centerfold game. I posed for photos as you cued me to charm you with my words.

"My likes are . . . the smell of wool when it gets wet, pulling a perfectly browned Beef Wellington from the oven, the word *soliloquy*."

"Dislikes?" you asked, Nikon clicking away.

"Cacophonous jazz horns, ringing phones, gray spots in a banana."

Then you would go, your likes never failing to include "new discoveries," and your dislikes always the same: boredom, running out of ketchup, people who say *I beg to differ*.

I couldn't comprehend the intricacies of your PhD program, tripping over the riddles of terms like *applied physics*. But I understood when you swore your research would launch you to the top, that I could be the half that made you whole, that together we would make a life lesser people could only envy. I laughed as I imagined the future us. It was so easy to feel happy then. Other people leapt at the fresh start of a new year. I reveled in the rebirth of a clean basket of laundry, or trash day, the cleansing gift of having my stinking mistakes carted away by strangers.

When we couldn't stay in bed forever, we suffered the adjustment of finding things to do together out in the world. That's when you shared a past time of yours called "B&E."

"Breaking and entering. Penal Code 459." You explained with a smirk that when the Lawrence Berkeley Lab issued your key, they inadvertently gave you a master to every building on campus.

Ten minutes later we peered over the edge of the flat black roof of Barrows Hall, clouds hovering above as if contemplating our presence on that expanse of asphalt, knowing we didn't belong there. That's where you first lectured me on Sir Isaac Newton, explaining how every object continues in its state of rest or straight uniform motion unless external forces compelled it to change. As a political communications undergrad this was new information to me, and I bathed in the sun of your brilliance while you eyed the nude women sunning themselves on the gym patio nine floors below. Squinting against the brightness, your eyes rested on an anorexic girl stretched out alone on a towel, the sharp edges of her bones visible even from a distance. The sight of her body frightened me somehow and I wanted to escape that view but you were still staring.

"I always wonder how a girl like that fucks," you said, your voice barely a whisper.

Looking back, maybe this should have been a warning. But I was so close to the edge of that flat roof I felt dizzy, like some magnetic force in the sky wanted to pull me off. This of course was a time when I couldn't tell the difference between paranoia and plain good sense. Even with all that's happened, I still think about those early days of our enchantment with something resembling fondness. Mostly though, I think about the past year.

I know I came a bit unhinged, but in my defense, you could have been more supportive last May. I can still hear the front door slamming, followed by the tranquil footsteps of a man who believes he has returned to the quiet sanctuary of an empty house. I still feel the tiny pulse of surprise as your senses registered that your showroom of a home was not in fact vacant but occupied by a glazy eyed woman planted on your

Natuzzi couch, cat curled on her lap, watching Oprah give stuff away on TV. I can still feel your body register shock that this woman on the couch was your wife, the esteemed Communications Director for the mayor of America's twelfth largest city.

"What are you doing home?" Your voice pitched with alarm as your eyes scanned the scene, absorbing the incongruity of daytime television, flannel pajamas and Ketel One. "Are you sick?"

I unglued my eyes from the television to look at you. "I got fired."

"You got *fired*?" Your adam's apple bobbed as you swallowed.

"I made a typo."

"You made a *typo*?"

You went on like this, repeating my words like some hysterical fucking Mockingbird until I handed you the press release.

Your voice quavered as you read the title aloud. "City Council Shits On Mayor's New Policy."

"It was supposed to say *shifts*." I pummeled a pillow with my fists as the cat leapt off my lap. "*Shifts, Shifts, Shifts!*"

"This went *out*?" Your eyes widened as your adam's apple wobbled again.

"I'm a laughingstock." My chin puckered as I started to cry, softly at first, then long jagged wails. "No one will ever forget this."

Your answer to my sobs was to press the heels of your palms to your forehead and say "Wow," over and over again. I knew I had fallen in your eyes, that image meant everything, and fifty percent of the power couple your mind held on a gleaming marble pedestal had vaporized. It wasn't fair. I'd just gotten distracted. I was spending hours on the phone talking to doctors, foolishly believing when they promised my father would be fine, even when my eyes told me otherwise. Losing twenty pounds in a month couldn't be good for anyone. A body may grow lighter but the man inhabiting it grows heavy with defeat.

I stopped blubbering long enough to down a shot of vodka, then another. I felt better numbed and fuzzy at my edges. I realized then how consonants change lives. A shift turns to shit, friends turn to fiends, Native Americans with their proud heritage become naïve Americans, an epidemic. My mind flew in an endless loop, listing all the better mistakes I could have made.

Thus began my Period of Decline, as you later labeled it. In the dull glow of your disapproval I slouched in bed slurping coffee and watching you get ready for work, work that promised glory and even more money than you had already made selling that patent I couldn't pronounce. I had fired off sixty resumes, determined to regain my status in the world, but didn't receive a single response. I lowered my standards, decided to settle for anything halfway decent, emphasized flexibility in salary as my key selling point, and still – *Zilch. Goose egg. Nada.*

We commenced a daily exchange, you sliding inside our room from the Madagascar maple wood closet like an actor appearing from stage left, looping your tie into a knot I had begun to wish was a noose, asking in that tone laced with disgust, what did I plan to do with my day? I couldn't wait for you to leave those mornings but when you turned to go I grasped your thigh in a hug like a weepy two year old battling the injustice of being dumped at day care. "I love you. Do you love me too?"

You cleared your throat. "Of course. Yes." Your voice held all the conviction of a hostage gripping a newspaper before his hollowed chest, reciting the script demanded by intransigent captors.

After a few months of my moping, you suggested I find a hobby. "Why not get busy on that backyard? Get us a landscape design going?"

Together we had built a house dazzling enough to serve as proof of our own everlasting beauty, our abiding newness, our modern thinking bright as the light from sconces radiating across buttermilk walls. Our blank gaping eyesore of a backyard was the final step in finishing our home but was put on hiatus when I got canned. It didn't interest me anymore and you were furious about it, a fact revealed every time your eyes landed on that dull chalky ground the texture of moon rock.

I never told you this, but by then I already had a hobby of sorts. I'd taken up jogging. It began as a test to see whether old Sir Isaac was telling the truth, whether a body in motion really stayed in motion, or whether the old man was full of shit. But soon I forgot my experiment and the runs just became about the stories I heard. Stringing together words overheard on my path through the park, I pieced together tales of carefully constructed lives, lives doused with equal parts monotony and catastrophe.

Stepping outside the morning of my first run, a woman glided past me walking backwards, one ham-hock bicep pumping while the other pressed a cell phone to her ear and she yelled into it, describing her breakfast in number of points consumed. At the canyon bridge, a pair of sixty-something men moved toward me, their bodies adorned with Nike swooshes, hands gripping mocha lattes. Running past them, I stole a slice of their conversation. "You know –the one whose daughter fell down a flight of stairs and ended up dead?"

That was all I took before brushing past them, and in my mind I saw a wispy haired toddler whose father spoon fed her applesauce from a jar as mine had done, who cut her juice in half with water so she wouldn't get hopped up on sugar, a girl whose father drove a Volvo for its safety ratings as mine had, a miniature family who did everything right but still got tackled by misery.

At the fountain I reached a woman singing, upturned fedora at her feet. Short and round with skin the color of cinnamon, she had a voice clear and pure as mountain rain. *What would you think if I sang out of tune? Would you stand up and walk out on me?* Her voice reached inside my chest, wrapping itself around my heart, gripping it until I almost couldn't breathe. I knew with a cold certainty I had never before possessed that someone had in fact stood up and walked out on her, a someone she never expected to do such a thing, and that this person's leaving had put tears in her voice.

Passing her, I reached a man whispering to a little girl dressed head to toe in Pepto-Bismol pink, *Shhhhh*, the birdie lying limp in the sidewalk was asleep and she shouldn't touch. In the distance a dog barked, then a man barked, *Shut it.* Then I looped around the bell tower and headed back to where the woman with the liquid voice had started *Fifty Ways To Leave Your Lover.* I wound up back home, panting and gasping for breath, marveling that despite all I'd witnessed my life remained exactly the same as when I'd left.

Drained from running in circles, plucking terror from the ordinary, I reclined across the width of our bed. I closed my eyes, let my mind wander. I thought about women who pick up hitch-hiking men, tried to remember the rules to the TV game show *Truth or Consequences*, wondered if there's a name for the phobia where you fear the passage of time. The one where you're deathly afraid all the good times have passed and now all that remains is the work of trying to be happy. Then my mind flew to suffering, how we try so hard to avoid it, how in the end that probably makes us suffer more. I fell asleep and woke with a start, forgetting where I was. Then, in a flood of sound the voice of the woman singing in the park returned to me and I feared she had looked inside me, that she had seen my life with the clarity of a prophet.

I never thanked you for coming with me to visit my Dad when he got so sick last October, when the cold sliced through what otherwise might have been an endless summer. We never got around to discussing this, but decorating for Halloween in the ICU is tricky, isn't it? Cardboard skeletons are a no-no since so many patients resemble skeletons themselves, and ghosts seem in poor taste, hovering reminders of souls who passed on the premises, often right before the eyes of those still struggling to survive. I always felt the better choices were grinning green witches, or the goofy gap-toothed pumpkins rotting from the inside out, just like people.

My father never liked you, though he was too kind to let you know it. He told me the first night you met, when he visited me at Berkeley. I had spent all day making Boeuf Bourguignon to impress you. Over dinner, my father nodded as you talked about yourself, describing your research in painful detail. Then he stayed after you left to help clean up the huge mess I'd made. Up to his elbows in dishwater, he stared out the window over the sink, speaking as if to himself. "So full of shit his eyes are brown," he mumbled, shaking his head. "A guy who'll piss down your back and tell you it's raining."

I wanted to be there when my father died, but when the buzzers on one of his machines went haywire, the ICU staff shooed me away. You worked late at the lab on his last night, so I took refuge alone in a box-like waiting room awash in carpet the color of Windex and lit only by the glow of a flickering television. Later I churned the wheels of my mind backward, calculating that it was just after *Friends* and in the early throes of *Judge Judy* when he died. So enthralled was I with the plaintiff's case, I didn't even hear the Code Blue.

Afterwards, the light inside his room felt dimmer. The hospital must do that on purpose so we don't see how quickly skin changes from the color of someone barely living to the color of someone not living at all. I said goodbye to my father's corpse, stupidly unable to kiss him, barely able to rest my fingertips on his bony shoulder. I worried he would come to life beneath my lips like in the fairy tales he read to me forty years earlier, knowing even as I recognized that fear how asinine it was, because wouldn't that be a good thing? For him to snap open his lids, widening his eyes in mock terror, singing "Gotcha!" I'd be mad for a split second, then I'd laugh and say, "Oh you! You really had me there!" The nurses would chuckle shyly, accomplices in his elaborate prank.

Instead of kissing him I just stood there and said in a voice so thin it barely existed, "Bye, Dad." Limbs numb, I shuffled outside to the parking lot. The automatic sliding doors sucked closed behind me for the last time and the wind hit my face, crisp as an open-handed slap.

I couldn't bring myself to call you until I'd driven to my father's house and dialed the few living friends remaining in his outdated Rolodex. Instead of pulling a card from the spindle and throwing it away when someone died, my father crossed out the entire card and scrawled across one line of the X, *DEAD*. I pronounced my news several times, picturing the person attached to the voice on the other end of the line reaching for a pen and making their own notation on a card holding my father's name.

At our makeshift wake that night, none of us could cry but you, remember? You sat rocking in my father's chair at the edge of his miniature living room, mouth leaking the anemic words people say in the aftermath of death like, "I can't believe he's gone." Even in the tangled ropes of my grief I found this amusing, how the person arguably least connected to the dead man appeared the most torn up, at least on the outside. But your pain was genuine and that touched me. It's a moment that made me believe it was right to marry you, a moment I would place onto a small pile, something to draw upon and sustain me in the coming months.

It was November when I found out. You were working late again and I stood alone in our kitchen making a smoked mozzarella and radicchio risotto. The recipe takes forever because you have to introduce the broth into the rice a cup at a time so it can absorb slowly. Dumping in too much at once ruins it.

So I flipped on the TV for company and there you were. With her. You and your skin and bones lab assistant at a Celtics game, in what looked like pretty expensive seats, shoving your tongue down her emaciated throat for the Kiss-o-Cam. It was rather brazen of you. But I also see why you never expected to get caught. I loathed basketball and recent events had left me fresh out of family and friends. So how would I ever know?

I hit record and preserved what can only be deemed an epic kiss, impressive work by anyone's standards. Then I hit rewind and played it in slow motion, daring myself to believe that was really you on the screen lapping at the mouth of a near skeleton. I thought of all the other things I'd seen, my failure to entertain the questions they had posed. The working late, the vastly improved personal hygiene, a sudden motivation for push-ups. Simon and Garfunkel said a man hears what he wants to hear, but I think that applies to women too. I remembered then the woman singing in the park, how she had tried to warn me.

This of course was before your lab Christmas party, the night my flaws and deficiencies became a matter of public record. My conduct was unimaginative, I know. It was just after that Tiger Woods mess and while having the gray bleached from my hair I read in *People* that Tiger's pathetically trusting and ruthlessly deceived wife had beaten the shit out of his SUV (using Tiger's own golf clubs!) when she learned of his infidelities. I closed my eyes, breathing in the chemicals burning at my scalp, envisioning the release poor Mrs. Woods must have felt, a cleansing catharsis of rage. Seldom in this life do we get to do what feels good, what we ache for in the moment, perhaps because what we yearn for is so often inappropriate, or in my case, illegal.

But lack of originality aside, I need you to understand why I wound up in our unlandscaped backyard with a baseball bat that night. Nibbling from the buffet at your party, I spotted your mistress poised in lively conversation with another physics geek, sipping from a tiny bottle of Perrier. I almost didn't recognize her, clad as she was in something other than a stiff white lab coat, suckling at something other than your stiff white cock. Then you approached her, placed your palm on the small of her back and spoke something in her ear that made her smile. The sight of this small intimacy triggered so much angst I couldn't stand to be inside my own skin. So I commenced the feat of drinking my body weight in vodka, steeling myself against all that I knew, and as my father would have said, "That's when the wheels came off."

After the party as we pulled inside the garage, I spotted your Louisville Slugger resting against the wall and thought, *That's it!* I felt such salvation knowing I could do something to feel better, even if that something was temporary. I grabbed that bat and ran through our house, out the gleaming floor-to-ceiling sliding glass door, a door where so many sparrows had believed they were flying through an endless expanse of blue sky until they hit their own reflection in the glass, snapping their tiny unsuspecting necks.

Outside in the cold, I slammed that goddamn bat into the almost frozen ground. It wasn't like smashing your SUV but still, the violence of it, the shuddering reverberation through every nerve of my body as the unyielding ground interrupted my swing —it felt exquisite. The sound of an expensive bat colliding with the earth became a symphony, a soundtrack to accompany my paroxysm of rage. Through our bedroom windows, I saw my little Siamese curled up on the floor next to our bed, watching my body absorb every impact. I imagined her understanding precisely what I was doing out there and why. She had, after all, witnessed the past eight months. Cats are intuitive creatures and a goldfish could have comprehended what was brewing in that house.

Still pounding the ground, my mind shifted to my father and I inexplicably remembered the only time he had ever raised his voice at me. He was wound up, livid because another employee had filed a complaint against him, something the post office called a Grievance. I thought he said Grief Ants and imagined colonies of sad insects crawling over me, stinging my skin with their bites, infecting me with despair. My father was in middle management, which he counseled was the worst hell to be in because it meant always being stuck. Being caught in the middle was the worst position to be in, he warned. I was never to let that happen, did I understand that? he yelled. Yes, I said, eyes on my plate, arranging peas so they wouldn't touch my meatloaf.

I muttered to myself through what I thought was a soft rain, realizing only later when the policeman commented on the condition of my face that the soaking came from my own tears. I didn't hear myself, but I suppose my muttering turned to screams and I somehow wandered into the neighbor's backyard with my bat. I cried the same words over and over until that nice young cop with the dimples disarmed me, prying my whitened fingers from the neck of that bat as he cooed soothing sounds. His report said I was screaming *Grief Ants!*

Looking back, I see I lost my mind. I've worked so hard to get it back, no thanks to the hours spent on the scratchy beige couch of Dr. Shellac where he forced us to pivot our bodies toward one another and speak back and forth like obedient children, faking inspiration from his insipid little prompts.

After the baseball bat incident you baffled me with your declaration that you loved me, not her. You insisted we see a counselor who quoted $250 per hour, then we sat in his office, jaws clenched, backs erect, eyes roaming the room, studying the furnishings and deeming it the décor of a therapist who should charge much less. We pronounced this judgment in whispers to one another, staring at our watches, wondering when our session would start before we learned $250 bought not a full hour, but a mere fifty minutes of therapy. I declared victory about the furniture: We agreed on something! And you even smiled at the nickname I'd given this shrink for his hairsprayed coif! Therapy was working already! But as you know, things unraveled from there.

"Jack, tell Leslie something you like about her," Shellac commanded in that patrician voice of his.

You paused for a long time, stumped by that one. I watched as the wheels turned inside your mind and felt your body heat rise as you registered a long overdue comprehension of how an animal might chew off its own limb to free itself from a trap. Had this session been a game show, an oversized clock would have begun ticking in time with a message flashing onscreen: *Bonus round! No penalties for clichés!* As you remained mute, a buzzer would have sounded, triggering a collective groan from the studio audience. Our host Dr. Shellac would have spoken in a tragic voice, "I'm sorry Jack, but the answer we were looking for was *Beauty. Brains. Compassion.* Other acceptable answers would have been *Strength. Humility. Courage.*"

Game show Shellac dissolved before my eyes, replaced once again by therapist Shellac who always seemed to play favorites, dropping you hints when you clearly hadn't come prepared.

"Jack, it seems you want to say something."

After wasting a good five minutes of therapy time ($25 worth of dead air!) you finally cleared your throat.

"Ummm…" Your fingers dug into the arm of the couch as I waited, holding my breath. "She's a really good cook."

Shellac lapsed into a silence that I shall take the liberty here of characterizing as *stunned*. I lapsed into the non-silence that you yourself called *apoplectic*. You and Shellac snapped to attention, scrambling to calm me, but some words guarantee to only trigger more rage. *Relax. Whatever. Get over it.*

In marriage counseling there exists an implicit contest to win the sympathies of a supposedly neutral mediator —to get them on your side, to make them comprehend all the bullshit you've endured at the hands of your partner, to see that you are truly the blameless party. Walking in there I figured I had this won hands down, but as I stood up to march out of Shellac's office that afternoon, I gasped in alarm, jabbing my finger at the title of a book displayed on his shelf, *The Rapist's Guide To The DSM IV.*

"No," Shellac said in a voice trained to appease. Threading an index finger beneath the words on the spine, Shellac showed me I had misread. The book's title was *Therapist's Guide To The DSM IV.* I felt your eyes rolling behind me and Dr. Shellac taking mental notes, wondering, what else has this hysterical bitch misread? My eyes kept playing tricks on me in those days. Words on the page said *pinning* but I saw *pimping*. An article discussed the workforce, but I saw work*farce*. "Crazier than a rat in a tin shithouse," my father would have said.

So I understand why I wound up seeing Dr. Shellac all on my own, but I wanted you to finally know the things I learned in his sessions. Shellac taught me that:

"Losing your job can be traumatic."

"Losing your father can be traumatic."

"Learning your husband has been fucking his lab assistant can be traumatic."

He also told me that people have compared both job loss and the betrayal of an affair to the grieving process of death, glossing over what comparisons are made in the event of all three occurrences happening nearly simultaneously. Then Shellac taught me the stages of grief: denial, anger, bargaining, depression and some other one I can't remember now. Frankly, I had stopped paying attention by then. While Shellac nattered on about the groundbreaking discoveries of Dr. Kubler-Ross, I gazed outside the window, staring at a single fox sparrow huddled on the leafless branch of a birch, its body puffed up against the chill. It reminded me of Berkeley, the first time we shared a winter sky, our eyes watching the clouds rearrange themselves as they prepared to storm. You sang *Baby It's Cold Outside*, rocking me softly and kissing my hair, thrilling me with how you switched voices on a dime, creating the illusion of a real duet.

By then I didn't need Shellac anymore. I had my own form of therapy. Remember all those nights I slept in the guest room? I'd become addicted to horror novels. *The Shining, The Exorcist, It.* I was ravenous for the suffering of others, calmed in the knowledge that things could be worse. I read until the words blurred and jumped off the page, scrambling themselves like they did everywhere else. Then when I still couldn't sleep, I passed the early morning hours with crosswords, peering at the newsprint through new prescription glasses, pencil poised in hand and asking myself, what's a five letter word for failure? What's a four letter word for regret?

The last time you came home I wanted to talk about the secret games of words, their incongruities, how they liked to trip us up, little pranksters wreaking havoc in our lives. I wanted to talk about subtleties that make English the most difficult language to learn. Like being too close to the door to close it, how quicksand works slowly, how oversee and overlook are opposites. I got myself pretty wound up. You were shaking me by the shoulders when I fired off what would be my final observation.

"You got laid. I got laid off. One's good, the other's bad. Get it?"

I was just trying to have a sense of humor, to laugh at my own misfortune, which if you ask me is pretty goddamn mature. But you resisted playing along, refusing me so much as a smile, instead putting on your grumpy face and saying in that tone one reserves for a puppy who pissed on the rug, "We need to talk."

The end of a marriage is about a lot of things I suppose, but for me it's about humiliation. Not humiliation like when I think of you choosing her over me. My disgrace stemmed from trying so hard to win you back, from the oodles of money I wasted on lingerie, the *Mastering the Art of the Blowjob* DVD for which I paid rush shipping charges. My abasement was in spreading my legs on the plush chocolate colored carpet of our home theatre, a room I selected for its black-out shades, its dimness a smokescreen through which you might desire my creping forty-something skin. The scene in that room is one of many that will rest forever in the photo album of my mind, complete with its caption, "Here's me. Begging him to fuck me."

When you announced you were leaving, that you could no longer deny your love for your scrawny but brilliant colleague, you spoke as you would to a store clerk, a customer trading in the durable appliance that served well for many years but no longer stacked up to the modern model with its shiny amenities. Realizing I'd played the Charlie Brown to your Lucy, letting you snatch the football away again and again, I tuned out the rest of your briefing. I only heard your voice going *yappity yappity yappity*, and I marveled how you never appreciated the economy of words and reminded myself that you always had to get the last one in. *Yap*.

By the way, I did a little Wikipedia research on Dr. Kubler-Ross myself, a real Miss Smarty Pants if you ask me. What Dr. Dipshit neglected to mention in his $250 lectures was that *the steps are not meant to be complete or chronological*. He neglected to explain that *some people may get stuck in one stage*. So if this is true, what's the point of having stages at all? What's the point of naming them? In my previous letters I wanted you to know why I got so stuck in *anger*. I needed you to comprehend why I was driven to sharpie *Selfish Prick* on your lab coat. I didn't want to be the kind of woman who sharpied people's lab coats, even if those people deserved it. I was so desperate for you to understand, but at this point I no longer give a shit what you think.

I finally understand that a lot of what happened is my fault. When we wrote our vows, I kept mine pragmatic, careful not to over-reach. I spoke of true partners sharing intertwined lives, best friends with benefits and crap like that. I forgot to throw in words like *trust, devotion, forever*. If I reached further maybe I would have gotten more. That was my mistake. I also think marriage vows should contain the word *scapegoat*. Because what is a spouse but someone you can blame for all that has gone wrong in your life? Money squandered, cities unexplored, the disastrous duvee and bedroom lamps? Getting married means putting all your eggs in one basket, putting your chips down on one number, betting it all and standing back to hope for the best. No one tells you that most of married life consists of the boring stuff, sheer drudgery peppered by a few solid tragedies that make you wax nostalgic for the dull days. You stand scratching your head realizing that *Endless Love* has become *Loveless End*, an anagram of your vows, and you look at your life feeling something akin to buyer's remorse. You start out wanting to be saved by love and in the end just hope you can survive it.

I'm going to wrap this up now because Gmail is eavesdropping, offering volume discounts on Zoloft, assortments of lawyers, and something called *Satisfy Your Man*. This note should be my last. Think of it as my sentimental send-off, like a message scrawled in the high school annual of someone you spent half your life with but now realize you'll probably never see again. I do want you to know that after the Kubler-Ross debacle, I decided it was time to rely on myself for a change. I did my own research and learned you left something out that day on top of Barrows Hall, quoting laws of physics like you'd invented them yourself. You neglected to share Newton's third law, the law I had to discover the hard way. You failed to mention that when two bodies interact, their force might be equal, but they will always push in opposite directions, their natural friction propelling them away from each other. Knowing this was our fate made me feel better and for the first time in as long as I can remember, the world almost makes sense. Giving up on the impossible isn't so difficult. Instead it's like my father used to say, "The great thing about beating your head against the wall is that it feels so good when you stop."

Love,

Me

DIFFERENT BUT THE SAME

When we were kids, Mundo Gavaletti and I played "The Price Is Life" with lizards caught from a canyon bordering the apartments where we lived with our mothers. We imprisoned the contestants in a King Edward cigar box, then wrested out a scaly body and placed the player at his mark. Each lizard was presented with a question selected from our own version of current events like, Why did a Chicago Seven defendant call the judge a fascist dog? Or, What did Charles Manson name the coming apocalypse?

If our contender responded correctly, he won the gift of life. As the game show host, I congratulated him in my studio audience voice, escorted him to the canyon rim and watched him race like hell into the brush. If a player was incorrect, a buzzer sounded deep in Mundo's throat, signaling me to release the blade from our homemade guillotine. Once the head was severed, we watched the body flop on searing asphalt until it fell still. Since lizards can't talk, odds were stacked against them, their fate controlled by higher beings consisting of Mundo and me. But those lizards played along, grateful probably for the illusion of a real chance.

Mundo lived in the building next to ours, in the Pitford Arms Apartments. Mundo called them The Armpit Apartments, because the complex was shaped like an armpit, among other reasons. Each building had eight units, four on top, four on bottom, with walls the color of rotting chocolate. Stucco on the dusty outer hallways swirled into jagged edges so when you slid against them in a fight, the scrape burned to your skin. Those halls reeked of Colt 45 and stale cigarettes and if I stayed in them too long, my nose exploded in sneezes.

But living next door to Mundo isn't how I came to know him. Our mothers were both divorced and had to pawn us off on someone during that remnant of time between the end of school and the end of a shift at Piper's Coffee Shop. So it was in 1969, just after my sixth birthday, that Mundo and I met at Mrs. Mallow's. About the same time Mrs. Mallow learned she couldn't survive on her monthly $200 from Social Security, she noticed swarms of kids and lone young mothers inhabiting the apartments around her and reinvented herself as a childcare specialist. Mrs. Mallow had a nose even a man would regret and a smell so sour I couldn't stand next to her. But every day after school, I walked to her one-bedroom apartment where I was caged with fifteen other kids until our mothers came to collect us, sweaty, exhausted, and very aware that other people in other places were living much better lives.

My first day in her living room, Mrs. Mallow ushered me to a boy named Edmundo and announced that we were the same age. Under her logic, this meant we were supposed to play together, "like little gentlemen." Edmundo's hair, shiny and black as oil, hung down to cover most of his brown face until he flung his head back, unveiling eyes that could flash to black in an instant. We both wore Toughskin jeans and T-shirts bought on sale at K-Mart.

"Call me Mundo," he said, and didn't ask for my name.

After we met, Mundo and I shared our brief life stories. I went first: 1968, age 5, my Aunt Teresa stares down into my green eyes, admires my golden curls and long, thick lashes and says, "You're too pretty to be a boy," scarring me for life. 1969, age 6, my father packs two paper grocery sacks with all of his worldly possessions, slaps my mother one last time and heads toward the door. As I start to cry, he stops in the doorway, turns to me and says, "See ya later champ."

Mundo's story was similar, except that Mundo's mother had ejected his father from their apartment for some unknown transgression, calling him a shit-sucking bastard as he stumbled out their door. I learned fast that Mundo was a loyal, protective, wickedly imaginative friend. We scratched our names in soft wet cement, played bloodthirsty games of Cowboys and Indians, and picked fights with younger, less feral boys. We became inseparable.

Mundo's mom was the first lesbian I ever knew. Mundo didn't call her "Mom," and I never called her "Mrs. Gavaletti." She was Dana, to me, Mundo, and everyone else in the Armpit Apartments. I didn't think much of it when a tall, horse-faced woman named Xan moved into their apartment two years after I met Mundo, other than feeling a little depressed over Dana's corresponding decision to cut her hair. I never would have confessed it to Mundo, but before Xan came, I had sort of a crush on Dana. I felt a tiny thrill in those rare moments that she bent down and brushed my blonde hair out of my eyes. The touch of her fingers against my forehead triggered a sensation I'd never known, a tingling I knew was probably wrong to have when Mundo's mother touched me. But Dana's hair had been the cornerstone of my crush, falling past her shoulders in thick dark waves. When it disappeared, so did the tingling. Dana said the cut was the new style and called a "shag," but it morphed her hair into a dull mousy brown, sticking to her head in all the wrong places, turning her into a butch David Cassidy.

I asked Mundo what he thought of Dana's new hair and he shrugged his shoulders, not looking up from the Tonka eighteen-wheeler he was edging up the wall of his room. I asked what he thought of Xan and he released the truck, letting it crash to the floor. "Who the fuck cares what I think?"

Mundo's upper lip quivered in a snarl and I froze until he bent down to pick up the toy and continued scraping its wheels against the walls. I busied myself with my own rig and we played in silence until dark and I heard my own mother outside, hollering for me to help carry in some groceries.

For my eighth birthday, my mother gave me a package of green army men. I had asked for a bike, the kind with the sparkly banana seat and tall handlebars, but knew better than to expect to get it. Mundo and I poured the tangling of bodies onto a corner of concrete next to the dumpster in the Armpit parking lot and played war under a blistering L.A. sun. We made a good effort, scratching our throats raw with machine gun blasts, whistling out bombs that sailed down for catastrophic explosions, but we got bored fast.

"This isn't realistic." Mundo threw down a gunnery sergeant in disgust.

"I know, it sucks." I stared down at the stoic expressions on men crouching with machine guns or lobbing grenades and fingered the softness of the tiny white flag held by the soldier nearest me.

"War should be hell. Like Vietnam, you know? Everybody screaming and dying and shit. Gooks jumping out of nowhere, killing your buddies right before your eyes. Bombs should explode, burning dudes alive so they're screaming, *Fuck, man! I'm on fire!*" Mundo danced the parking lot, arms flailing like he was engulfed in flames, then twisting and writhing until he finally wound down to die in front of me.

"I know," I repeated dumbly.

"Wait here," Mundo said, jumping back up.

He reappeared minutes later with lighter fluid and matches borrowed from Apartment 8C's hibachi and doused everyone from the platoon leader to the recon team with Kingsford. We leaned in to watch the men as Mundo tossed the match —our version of a napalm bomb—on the unsuspecting troops. A breathy *Houummfff!* sound flew up and I reeled back from the rush of heat.

"Fucking cool!" Mundo screamed, flames reflecting in his black eyes.

We watched the men burn to their deaths in an inferno of orange and green, leaving nothing but a smear of wax and chemical fumes. I looked around then to check for adults who might yell at us, but there weren't any. We enjoyed our fire awhile longer, burning carefully selected garbage until we got bored again and stomped out the flames. I looked to Mundo, ready to hear what he felt like doing next. His face looked wrong. Too innocent and too bland.

"What's wrong with your face?" Mundo demanded while I still stared at him, struggling to figure out what wasn't right.

The fire had singed off our eyelashes and eyebrows, leaving soft empty patches of baby skin. With our faces robbed of expression, no one could tell anymore what we were feeling inside. Our faces no longer betrayed our furious doubt and the temporary blankness was a gift we wore like a super power. It didn't occur to either of us that we could have burned our own faces off, mutating ourselves into the monsters from movies on Channel 5. We were just trying to defeat the restlessness that hovered over us like a curse.

Ours was a tough neighborhood, with wolfish packs of teens who amused themselves by tackling younger kids and swinging them by their ankles over second story railings, or sometimes worse. Mundo was small for his age, but scrappy, and because even thugs recognize raw fierceness, Mundo and I could strut down streets I never could have braved alone. Boys our own age in the Armpit Apartments killed time with more mild forms of amusement, doing what I assumed all boys did: We stood around, smoked Lucky Strikes and talked shit. Mainly that shit consisted of crude remarks about what we might do to the private parts of one another's sisters, mothers, grandmothers, etcetera, if given half the chance, one-upping each other until we ran out of smokes. The group playing this game was always the same: Teddy, the only one of us with two parents at home. Boris, a wispy-haired kid who spoke with a lisp that made him Borith. Tyrone, a round-faced kid whose brother came home from Vietnam without any legs. And pudgy Oscar, who begged to join the private escapades of Mundo and I until we dumped a box of rocks on him from a playground tree house after promising he could climb up with us, if he would first just stand beneath that tree, eyes closed and face tilted to the sky.

So it was just another summer day in 1973 when we all stood in the dusty halls of my building, trying to duck the stifling heat and playing the insult game. After Tyrone heard about his mother's ass and Boris took a healthy dose of abuse concerning his sister's lopsided breasts, Boris lobbed his own observation at Mundo.

"Tho what? Your puthy-eating Mama don't even like dick!"

Boris was echoed by the "OOOOooooh" that boys like us, who grew up in places like the Armpit Apartments, would sing after any halfway piercing crack, reliable as back up singers supporting their lead vocalist.

I could see from Boris's easy posture, the looseness of his shoulders, that he had no concept of his remark's velocity and had only flung it loosely in Mundo's direction as part of a frivolous boys' game. In a car accident, there's a split second before impact when the world and everything in it winds down to impossibly slow frames. Waiting for the force of the crash, knowing you're helpless to stop it, you're so terror-stricken by what's about to happen that time almost stands still. That's what it was like in the microseconds before

Mundo pounced on Boris, pummeling Boris's face with raging fists. Blood geysered from Boris's nose as he screamed for Mundo to stop. The rest of us climbed on Mundo's back, grabbing at this arms, but we couldn't hold them and he kept hammering Boris's face until the thick thumps of punches turned my stomach. We finally pulled Mundo off and I walked him away, leaving Boris bawling in a puddle of his own blood.

It was ludicrously unfair. Mundo had spoken far more vulgar words about other boys' mothers and everyone had just laughed and scuffed their feet. I realized then that Xan really bothered Mundo. Maybe it was the fact that they were lesbians, but I think Mundo was just jealous, craving a piece of the affection that Dana now hoarded for Xan. Before Dana met Xan, she sometimes had what Mundo referred to as "bad days," as in, "Dana's having one of her bad days. We should go to your place today." Most of those times, Mundo tried to stay out of Dana's way. Other days I stood by and watched as he cared for her as tenderly as a lover, shuffling to the couch with Styrofoam cups of Seagram's & 7Up, walking to the market, standing barefoot on the linoleum and scrambling eggs at a narrow kitchen stove no bigger than a toy.

"You have to eat something," Mundo would say, offering Dana a wobbling paper plate and freshly washed fork.

Dana would sit up and grasp the plate with both trembling hands, saying "Thanks, baby," as she stared zombie-like at a woman jabbering away on TV, the woman cheerfully unconvinced she could really wash cherries jubilee from a white blouse.

Whatever it was, I stood by and watched, helpless, as it got to Mundo. I saw him changing, hardening, leaving no softness inside at all. I felt myself losing him as he moved further away. Further away, but still stuck right there next to me in the Armpit Apartments.

I stayed the same. "Toughen up. Boys don't cry," my father had said when I fell out of a tree and broke my arm the week before he left us. I was still what my father would have called "pure pussy" inside, crying all over again the Sunday he called after three years of silence and promised to pick me up at noon for a Rams game. I spent three hours on the steps of our building, looking up every time a car turned the corner, but after three hours of strained hope, realized he wouldn't show.

With the soft worn dollars stolen from my mother's purse one at a time, I had saved up and bought a used Fender bass. It was the first thing I ever owned that I gave a shit about, possibly the last. I taught myself from the pages of *How To Play The Electric Bass*, a book the pawn shop clerk had thrown in for a quarter. Struggling with the chords, I dreamed I was John Paul Jones or maybe Steven Price. The Sunday my father ditched me for the second time, I imagined myself on stage, a million miles away from everyone, no longer holding my breath, no longer exhausted with yearning.

By the end of my seventh grade year, my mother managed to find her own new special someone, a pigeon-chested, gray-templed engineer named Jerald, who never wore anything without a stiff navy blue windbreaker. Underneath he wore crisp short sleeve shirts, their breast pockets clipped with two Bic pens, one red, one blue. I thought he was too old for my mom, too geeky and too ardent. But he was punctual for their dates and my mom started smiling a lot, something she hadn't done in a long time.

Jerald's presence in our lives needled me with angst. I wanted him gone, and at the same time dreaded the day he would inevitably leave. My uncertainty made me prickly and I sulked whenever he came over, refusing to engage his polite attempts at conversation, despite his careful focus of those efforts toward music, a topic he knew a lot about. On their seventh Friday night date in seven weeks, Jerald bought me my first album, a used copy of Led Zeppelin II. I made it a point to not say thank you.

Jerald walked down to the parking lot where his brother and sister-in-law waited to drive them all to see *One Flew Over The Cuckoo's Nest*. My mother still fidgeted in front of the bathroom mirror, putting on bracelets, then taking them off again. Finally she slammed her makeup drawer closed and bent down to hug me. "We won't be late," she promised.

"Don't think I don't know where you're going. Off to your little sex parties with the other pimps and whores." I felt my face twist to a sneer as the words bounced off my tongue. I meant to inflict pain, but once the words were out, I only wanted to pull them back in. I waited for the cathartic sting of a slap, but my mother didn't move. Her face melted into the expression of hurt surprise she'd worn every time my father hit her. She stared for a moment like she couldn't quite place me, then stepped to the door and slipped out without a sound.

As Mundo and I sat on the couch that evening in my sweltering apartment, the syllables of my words still lingered in the air, flying back to lodge in my throat, their sharp edges choking me. Mundo sensed my funk and produced two cans of Coors stolen from Dana's fridge, then flipped on the TV to giggle at Jimmy Walker mouthing off on *Good Times*.

I pulled out my bass and hit some notes, soft and guilty. I focused on the tougher chords, hitting them slowly, studying the position of my fingers compressing the strings, but my misery swelled inside my hands and I couldn't get anything right. Mundo told me to knock it off and watch the show.

At the commercial, he turned to face me. "Can you take a shit any time you want?"

I looked up from my beer. "Can I what?"

"You heard me."

"I never thought about it. Why?"

"Because I can't, that's why."

On the TV, Jimmy Walker bulged his eyes and shouted, "Dy-no-mite," cheered by a track of canned laughter.

"Can you go now, you think?" Mundo's own eyes bulged black, a warning I had come to recognize.

"Yeah, I guess. You want me to go?" I pointed to the bathroom.

"Hold it for awhile. It's almost dark. We'll go then."

I looked outside and watched as light leaked from the sky. Now that I had to hold it, all I could think about was how I had to go.

The show ended and Mundo announced that it was time. I locked the apartment and we stepped outside to a breeze that licked the fine layer of perspiration on my face. It was then that Mundo enlightened me that we were walking two blocks to where Jerald had left his Ford Mustang. I was to climb on top of the hood and defecate on the car.

"I don't know, man." I stared at Mundo, searching for a sign he was kidding. He wasn't.

"Come on. I'd do it myself but I can't. I'll watch out for you. It'll be fucking hilarious." Mundo bent at the waist, overcome with a high-pitched girlish laughter.

Two blocks over, I pulled down my Levi's and crouched on the Mustang's hood, shiny with the coats of wax I imagined Jerald applying in round, loving strokes. Maybe it was the position, or maybe the vision of Jerald's face when he realized what was on his car, but I couldn't go. Mundo hissed at me to get the hell off and climbed on the hood, mumbling about having to do everything himself.

"Turn around, you fag. I can't go with you staring at me like that."

I turned my back to Mundo, then swiveled around when he gave the okay, pausing to admire his work. Then the utter silence was shattered by a noise and we took off running.

"You're welcome," Mundo said, out of breath at my front door.

As I turned my key in the lock, it occurred to me that I had never complained to Mundo about Jerald. I wasn't sure I wanted Mundo thinking he could read my mind and I felt something black and flat and unnamable inside. Everything felt like too much, too fast. Things were changing all around me, I could see that. I just couldn't see how I fit into it anymore.

Jerald stopped coming around. Even in a polyester waitress uniform and orthopedic shoes, my mother was a knock out with ice blue eyes and skin I once heard someone compare to porcelain. But after Jerald, I don't remember a man coming by to take her out for so much as a cup of coffee.

Around this time, gangs started showing up in our neighborhood, recruiting easily with promises of security and acceptance, intangibles boys from the Armpit Apartments had never known. I came home late on a Friday night to find Oscar, still pudgy and eager to please, stepping from shadows in the dusty hall.

"Check it out," he said, lifting his shirt.

I looked at his waist, thinking he had a bag of weed or, knowing Oscar, just a pack of cigarettes pocketed from 7-11. But tucked between his waistband and rolls of fat belly was a gun. Something percolated inside me that I recognized as fear. Fear that someone like Oscar could have a gun in his pants. Fear that I didn't know what to expect anymore.

On my fourteenth birthday, Mundo told me to wait in front of my building, he had a surprise.

"And I won't keep you waiting," he called over his shoulder as he ran away from me, his own brand of slap at my father. Three minutes later, Mundo pulled up in a red Gran Torino with a white stripe, a car I of course knew belonged to the boyfriend of a woman across the street.

"Hop in."

I did as he said and we sped like maniacs through the streets of Los Angeles, whizzing left on Normandy down to West Third, turning again at Western Avenue until my head spun like the steering wheel and I quit wondering how Mundo had managed to get the engine started. Mundo and I grinned over at each other, tasting the freedom of being alone, together, in a fast car. We could go anywhere we wanted, disappearing forever. We could watch over each other like brothers and finally start our lives. Suddenly I missed my mom.

"No fucking way!" Mundo screamed when I suggested we head back home. Still small for his age, Mundo could barely see over the steering wheel as he flew past traffic on the right, making use of every fragment of open space at the curb. Little or not, he couldn't miss the LAPD cruiser that lit up behind us. Without a word, Mundo hit the gas, maneuvering like we were Starsky & Hutch, bouncing that Gran Torino over potholes and sidewalks as I fastened my seatbelt and gripped the armrest.

Just before we crashed into the back of a '69 Shelby and flipped into the front yard of a pink house on San Vicente Boulevard, Mundo squinted at me and drawled in his best John Wayne, "Out here, due process is a bullet."

Two days later I woke up on clean white sheets in the Good Shepherd Hospital, my mother whimpering softly in the green plastic chair next to my bed. I broke one leg, three ribs and suffered a moderate concussion. Mundo broke his collarbone and sliced open his forehead, leaving a cut that would form a scar shaped like half a lightning bolt. No one had insurance, so Mundo and I convalesced on the State of California's dime. My father didn't visit and I reminded myself I didn't care.

After a week, Mundo moved to the bed next to me and we spent our days cracking each other up with lewd remarks to nurses, a painful game because of my ribs. Afterwards, Mundo went to Juvy for six months. Nothing happened to me, except that my first day home, my mother actually tried to spank me. In spite of my crutches and bandaged ribs, she couldn't catch me and I laughed as she tried, crouching and circling me like an animal until she collapsed into tears all over again, slumping to her bedroom and closing the hollow door.

Mundo hadn't bothered to tell me that the week before my birthday outing, Xan had moved out and a thin, shapeless woman named Bobbi moved in. Mundo had started moving in directions too fast and too turbulent for me to keep up. Even before our crash, I knew it was a matter of not being sure I wanted to anymore. I started spending more time alone, playing my bass. I joined a band called "Hostile Angels" and started hanging with other guys in bands, guys who loved music and spoke of nothing else, guys who wanted to see their eighteenth birthday. The night Mundo came home from Juvy, I was out with my new set of friends.

Mundo and I never declared war, never called an end to our friendship, but by high school, it had ended just the same. On the way home from school one afternoon, I cut through the canyon where Mundo and I had once hunted lizards for a twisted boys game. Mundo loitered in the brush, smoking pot with a group considered burn outs even by Armpit standards.

"How's it goin'?" I said, trying to sound casual.

"How the fuck do you think it's goin'?" Mundo shot back, and the losers around him snickered as Mundo choked out smoke and added, "Little bitch."

I kept walking, half expecting to get jumped as I hurried past, but no one made a move.

I no longer had Mundo to protect me, so not long after that day in the canyon I did get jumped on the way home from practice. I wasn't hurt badly —a purplish black eye and the taste of my own blood when a fist slammed against my mouth—but it shook my mother up enough that she scrounged together a security deposit and we moved two weeks later. I started a new high school where I knew no one and no one knew me, and that was just fine.

Now I'm winding my way through my forties and when I write my age on a credit application, I feel like I must mean someone else. I have what most people would call a good life. A nice house, okay job, a wife who's not bad looking and a son of my own. I still play my bass, just never on stage like I planned and sometimes I wonder how I ever ended up here.

I heard a few years ago that Mundo got married. Two months after their wedding at the L.A. County Courthouse, Mundo came home to find his new bride on Mundo's sheets, taking it doggie-style from their next door neighbor. The fact that Mundo had a Glock 17 and paused to reload apparently complicated his public defender's ability to argue temporary insanity or heat of passion or whatever lawyers argue in those circumstances. Mundo got life for shooting his pretty young wife through the skull and then riddling her corpse with bullets. Had he not spared the neighbor, it would have been lethal injection.

I look at my life and think about Mundo and the other boys from the Armpit Apartments. Our stories were all different, but the same. Some of the other boys are in prison too and some work a cash register. I heard Oscar got murdered, but I don't know if that's true.

The first Sunday of every month, I drive my mother to our house for dinner. She's seventy-two now, but I still see a blonde in her early thirties, ripe with perilous beauty and I want to go back in time and tell that green-eyed boy with the long eyelashes who was me to straighten up.

"Whatever happened to that boy Mundo?" my mother asks out of the blue this Sunday, perched before a plate of chicken and mashed potatoes. "What a bad boy he was," and she tsk tsks, shaking her head. "I was so glad when we could finally move out of those apartments and get you away from him."

I want to defend him. He wasn't such a bad boy, I want to say. No worse than some. I can't bring myself to betray Mundo again, this time with the truth instead of desertion, so I shake my head.

"I don't know, Mom. Haven't heard a thing."

I've thought about going to see Mundo up in Folsom. I feel like I owe it to a boy who never stood a chance, but tell myself I don't have time to make the drive. If I'm honest, it's really just that I can't bear to see Mundo through a wall of smudged Plexiglas, his brown skin washed out, wearing one of those orange jumpsuits with "Lifer" stenciled in black on his back, a bulls-eye for the guards so they know Mundo for what he is. A guy with nothing to lose.

———

FIVE

My mother sleeps in spurts, twitching in her dreams, while I slouch at her bedside watching *Jeopardy!* The contestant I've named Science Dork is creaming the competition.

"This substance is attached to its shell by a pair of strands called chalazae."

Science Dork hits his buzzer. "What is an egg yolk?"

"That is correct!" Alex Trebek is jubilant.

It was recently pointed out that one of my problems is that I think I am smarter than I really am. So now I make it a habit to watch *Jeopardy!* to remind myself of all I do not know. The pre-packaged twenty-three minute dose of humbling holds the added benefit of drowning out the silence in this box of a room, a terrifying stillness interrupted only by the drone and hiss of an oxygen machine and my mother's ragged breathing.

———

A nurse called last month and informed me that my mother had been upgraded to Five. I interrupted mid-sentence. "Shouldn't it be called *downgraded?* My mother's been *downgraded* to Five?" The nurse ignored me and explained that a bed in Five had become available and my mother would be moved there immediately. The nurse didn't mention what event had caused a bed to become available.

At Mayfair Retirement Village, life has three levels. "Independent" living, "Assisted" living, and "Skilled Nursing," the last stop at the end of the road,

28

known at Mayfair by its building number, Five. When my mother moved to Mayfair two years ago, she started in Assisted Living and gave me unsolicited daily reports on her neighbors.

"Remember that woman Sonya? She sat at my table for meals?" My mother released a sigh and shook her head. "They had to put her in Five."

I had learned to brace myself whenever my mother prefaced a statement with, "Remember that man…?" Or "Remember that woman…?" Our last phone call had been, "Remember that nice young man Robert? The crippled one?"

"Yeah…" I held my breath.

"He died." Her voice was like a bullet to the chest.

This was the downside of living in a place like Mayfair. You built affections for the inhabitants of your little village, but then they died, departing with a punch to the stomach, another reminder of what lurked around the next curve. I had met some of the Mayfair residents at events choreographed for the families. There was Lillian, who had just turned one hundred and one and seemed more aware of her surroundings than I was; Edith, a former stage actress who thought Harry Truman was still President; and Robert, who was only sixty-six but looked a hundred because of the psoriatic arthritis that had attacked his spine and feet, leaving him, in my mother's words, "crippled." The word made me cringe. I thought about correcting her, educating her on politically correct terminology, but what was the point? You could say impaired, handicapped, vertically challenged, but when it came right down to it, they all meant the same thing. Words had different meaning at Mayfair Village anyway. When my mother called to report that her neighbor Jon was in rehab, I knew it was not the same kind of rehab I had just come from.

———

When the doctors pronounced my mother "very sick," I had shifted to a daily on our phone calls. I was still locked up in my own invented community of misfits then and couldn't leave for another sixteen days. But since my release back into the world, it had become more difficult to perform on those calls each night, nights when I only felt like curling into a fetal ball, maybe lifting my head to slurp from a glass of gin or wash down a pill, instead putting on a chipper voice to say, "Hi, Mom!" a voice that sounded so contrived to my own ears, I wondered why she couldn't hear it too.

———

I snap to attention now as my mother bolts upright in bed. "What's that goddamn cat doing here?" she screams.

"What?" I scan the shadows of the room like a fool. "There's no cat, Mom."

"You didn't bring Nader?"

"No, Mom. Nader's not here."

She squints at the corners of the gray-green room, unsure whether to believe me, then falls back against her pillow. After a moment, she seems to relax again, then closes her eyes. Nader was the Himalayan Siamese I had to put down last year when his kidneys failed, a cat mourned as deeply by my mother as by me. These outbursts set my heart racing, though I know it's just the Prednisone talking, the drug doctors prescribe when they don't know what else to prescribe, the drug my mother's been taking for weeks.

I tilt my face back toward the television where Alex Trebek is still going strong, and so is Science Dork.

"This four-letter chemical abbreviation refers to the rave drug, Ecstasy."

Now this one I happen to know.

"What is MDMA?" I whisper, and Science Dork echoes me onscreen.

Science Dork is tall and lean, and I catch myself wondering what he has tucked inside those Dockers and whether he knows how to use it. My mind wanders like this sometimes, because I haven't had sex in a year and there are parts of it that I miss. A year ago I was still married, still hanging by a thread to a life that didn't feel like mine, but a life nonetheless. One night my husband sat on the couch in his boxers watching *Jerry McGuire* on TV. I looked up from my book at the scene in the elevator where Renee Zellweger sees a deaf man sign to his girlfriend, "You complete me." I couldn't stop myself from saying out loud that if it were a movie about my life, and I had been the one signing in the elevator, the line would be, "You deplete me." The next morning my husband packed up and left, calling me "pathologically insensitive" as he walked out the door.

"Pathologically insensitive? That doesn't even make sense!" I had shouted after him. But later, staring at the empty space of rumpled sheets next to me, I worried whether it was better to be with the wrong man than no man at all. Some months later, after gliding down the slippery slope of self-medicating against my lopsided existence, I sat on a straight-backed metal chair in an antiseptic room two hundred miles from home. Across from me, a counselor sipped tea and asked, "Do you want to be right, or do you want to be in love?"

"I want to be right," I said, and the counselor winced.

—

Now I sit staring at the woman who is my mother and wonder how long it will be. When I think of her dying, both my parents gone, it seems important to remember my childhood, the only pure form of our time together. I think that if I can remember, I might understand how I got here, maybe even know what to do next. But when I try to remember, I can't. I only have pieces and don't even know if those pieces are real or imagined. My only memories spring from yellow tinted snapshots of a joy staged and impermanent, a Polaroid past that provides few clues for deciphering the present, except for the certainty that there was never a time when I felt comfortable inside my own skin.

The photos are a montage of birthday parties, pink frosted cakes, candles for wishes, and Barbie dolls with the price tags left on. There are Christmas trees, Easter eggs, and the uncle my mother warned me about each holiday, "Be careful. I think Uncle Ed touches little girls where he's not supposed to."

In an overexposed snapshot labeled by my mother's crooked handwriting, "Katy's B-Day – 1969," I stand rigid in our living room, a stiff blue taffeta dress confining me like a straitjacket. My hands are clasped behind my back in a pose manufactured by my mother, who had bent over me in irritation, manipulating my limbs like a mannequin while her burning cigarette bobbed between her clamped lips. "Say Cheese!" she sang, but in the photo my round face wears a deer-in-the-headlights expression. I knew that if I moved, even breathed, the picture could be ruined, and flashbulbs were expensive. My lips form a straight line, not the broad smile that would

31

serve as an exhibit, a piece of evidence establishing definitive proof of a happy childhood. "Why can't you just smile, for Chrissakes?" she had complained later, tossing the photo into a pile.

In the next photo it's summer at the beach, but instead of a bathing suit she has me dressed in a white t-shirt and navy blue polyester shorts that itched my crotch. Because the ocean was loaded with deadly creatures and riptides that sucked little girls out to sea, I couldn't go in. I posed at the shoreline, squinting into the sun, watching the other kids from the corner of my eyes as they shrieked with laughter, slapping the water as they jumped over tiny waves. But I knew better than to question my mother. It was like this everywhere. We didn't go to the snow —there might be an avalanche. After dark we stayed inside because the roads swarmed with drunk drivers then. At the mall, there were purse snatchers and perverts. Everywhere, danger lurked, and my mother wore herself out guarding against it. She was teacher; I was student. I paid attention and learned the lessons she taught so well.

In the photo labeled "Easter, 1970" my mother is forty-six, a year older than I am now. She stands at the kitchen counter, pressing cloves into a ham. Next to the ham is the blender in which she chopped cabbage for the cole slaw, the same blender she would later slip her hand inside when it didn't look like the blades were moving. But those blades moved fine, and she wrapped her hand in a paper towel that soaked to crimson as she screamed at me to go to my room and stay there. My father took her to get stitched up and when she returned, she berated me like I had told her to put her hand in the blender in the first place. "I could have lost my fingers!"

"Yeah, but you didn't," I said and her good hand sent me reeling with the sting of a slap.

"Bad things happen everywhere, so you have to be careful all the time. You can't let your guard down —not even for a minute." She shoved gauze-covered fingers in my face in case I'd missed her point. Sometimes, my mother's avoidance stemmed from sheer paranoia, a black abyss of neurotic fear. Other times, her instincts seemed spot on. Bad things could happen anywhere. Now it seemed even home wasn't safe.

"My job is to protect you. Understand?" That was her mantra, the words I heard when I wasn't allowed to attend sleepovers or go to sixth-grade camp. She did have lapses, inexplicable contradictions, like letting a five-year-old play with a stapler, or the night she disintegrated into a crazy woman after a fight with my father. She had mutated into an unrecognizable stranger, snapping, "Stop hanging on me, for Chrissakes!" when I wouldn't let go of her hand, then "Don't call me that!" when I looked up through eyes puddled with tears to whine, "Why, Mommy?"

I never forgot the flash of sheer hatred in her eyes, the eyes of a woman at the end of her rope. She taught me how to feel, how to fear, then recoiled, disgusted that I could be so high strung when she had sacrificed everything to give me the perfect life, a life painstakingly constructed out of safety and avoidance.

———

Photos of my mother showed her pensive, tense, a cigarette burning by her side, clenched between two slender fingers. In the only photo of us together, my mother stands next to me, one arm resting stiffly on my shoulder, the skin around her lips stretched back into a tight smile. I was responsible for her happiness and I was failing miserably. As I grew older, I had trouble talking to people, strained to make friends. What I lacked in personality, I made up for in smarts, but that got me into trouble too. "No one likes a smarty-pants," my eighth grade teacher scolded. So I learned to keep my mouth shut —most of the time. By high school, something dawned on me: my mother had no friends, and neither did I. We were wholly dependent upon each other for companionship. We played cards, watched TV movies, gave each other manicures, and baked the cookies, pies, and cakes that I devoured. I lived this way for years, straining between the comfort of insulating myself from the world, yet yearning for its gifts —even gifts that might bring pain. My mother guarded against the dangers I set in motion through my misguided desire to create something more. "Don't count your chickens, missy." "You can't win for losing." "Pride comes before a fall." The words hit with a thud. *She doesn't mean it, She doesn't mean it,* I whispered to myself over and over. I knew she didn't want me to get my hopes up, because that way I couldn't feel the burn of disappointment, the pain of loss. Her motivations were good, yet I hated her for those words and the thousands just like them, for instilling her doubts as my doubts, for making her fear my fear. Still, I counted no chickens, stayed out of the game, abandoned all aspirations for pride.

—

"I have to go to the bathroom," my mother announces.

This takes a long time. I help her sit up fully in bed, and we pause for a minute so she doesn't get too dizzy. Then, slowly, carefully, she puts her weight on the floor one foot at a time. She inches forward with her walker, me shuffling behind, grabbing at the air around her, thinking I can catch her if she falls.

At the toilet, she shifts her grasp from the walker, to me, to metal bars bolted to the walls. Her arms occupied, she looks at me and without a word I know to pull the white cotton underwear down her stick-like thighs, past her knees, all the way to her ankles. I try not to stare at the shriveled folds of thin skin covering her belly or the fireworks display of varicose veins creeping up her calves. Even with the photos in mind, it's hard to think of my mother as once having been young. So close to the body in which I grew, a body used and failing, I feel an awkward intimacy that makes me shy. I had shared that body, then clutched that belly and clung to those thighs. I step back to give her privacy and catch my reflection in the mirror. I will never be called beautiful, but sometimes when I glimpse my crooked nose, I pretend that I am. That nose is my mother's. It's the feature that tells the world I am her daughter. It's also the feature that once prompted my ex-husband to ask, had I ever broken my nose? I wondered now what my mother saw when she looked at me and if she ever searched my face and saw herself. Or did the person I had become, broken and biting, make that impossible?

—

We get her back into bed and she blows out another sigh.

"Kate?"

"Yes?"

"What is HD?"

"What is what?"

"HD! HD! What is it?" She is half screaming again, her voice pitched with irritation at my thick-witted response to a simple question. She seems to catch herself and asks again, softly this time, "What is it?"

I pause before answering, still uncertain. "It stands for High Definition. It's a TV broadcasting system. It's supposed to make the picture more clear."

"Oh." She settles back into the pillow and inhales deeply from the oxygen tube.

———

A week earlier, my mother's head turned on that pillow, and she looked at me, the lines of her face seeming to etch more deeply under the weak overhead light.

"I'm scared," she whispered, and she didn't have to say of what.

I want to save her from past and present both, erase her fear for good, but I don't know how. I want to go back in time and give her a new life, one without fear that the floor beneath her will collapse, fear that, in her case, may have been justified. It seems important now to finally understand the roots of the terror that had shadowed her for a lifetime, the doubt that made her search for the worst until she found it everywhere, the apprehension she had passed to me like a birthright. But in all my life, I never discovered more about her than bits and pieces. The first thing I had learned was that she couldn't swim.

"Really?" I had laughed at her. I thought she was joking, then realized by the shamed look on her face that she was telling the truth. But how could that be? Who didn't know how to swim? Next, I learned she couldn't ride a bike either. And then there was the matter of her teeth. I watched her soak the dentures she had worn since before she met my father, her lips curling in on her toothless gums as she scooped the dentures from a fizzy liquid and scrubbed them hard.

"What happened to your real teeth?" I had asked.

She gave me one of her standard shrugs, popped the dentures in place with two clicks, rinsed and spit and said to the bathroom mirror, "I guess they fell out."

As a child, I tried to break her past into manageable chunks, categorize it, force it into a sensible chronology, but I never could. My mother never detailed the excuses she made for her own mother, a woman who dumped her infant daughter at an unsuspecting neighbor's house in 1925 and disappeared, resurfacing five years later, standing on the porch with a new husband and a lipsticked mouth brimming with promises. From the fragments, I gathered that my grandmother liked men and liked to wear them out. She repeated her vanishing act four times before my mother turned thirteen, showing up out of the blue every few years with a new husband on her arm.

"It wasn't her fault," my mother coughed, saying all she would ever say about the worst thing you can do to a child. All evidence to the contrary, my mother swore her childhood was happy. Maybe it was, once she finally gave up waiting for her mother to be a mother.

———

"Kate." Her face tilts toward me on the pillow, her brown eyes flat and empty.

"Yes?"

"Whatever happened to that cute John Kennedy boy? They never talk about him anymore."

There's no easy way to say this, so I just say it. "He's dead, mom. Plane crash. Remember?"

"Oh."

———

Time and her place in it fluctuate now. Back in Assisted Living days, there were events to help mark the passage of time in a sunshine city where seasons are no help. I accompanied her to the Valentine's Day Ice Cream Social, Memorial Day barbecue, Fourth of July Picnic and in those long months before the holidays, formulated events like Country Western Day, where the more ambulatory residents could line dance to "Achy Breaky Heart." In Assisted Living days, I took her on outings. We went to the mall with her walker and portable oxygen tank for sales at J.C. Penney and lettuce wraps at

P.F. Chang's. We went to the yarn store, sometimes out for Sunday breakfast. Our roles had reversed completely by then, with me strapping her in under a seatbelt that her own hands were too shaky to operate, cautioning her to watch her fingers as I closed the passenger door and walked around to climb into the driver's seat.

My mother did not get the newspaper during the week, only Sundays. On one of our breakfast mornings, I fed a machine quarters and carried the heavy lump of newsprint back to our table. I slurped my coffee and watched my mother flip through the sections.

"What's new in the world?" I had been on a self-imposed news detox then, shielding myself, living by the creed that ignorance really was bliss.

"Oh, I don't know." She paused and her brown eyes rolled up to look at me from a face bowed in a familiar pose of shame. "I don't read the news."

I gave her a dubious smile. "Then what do you read?"

"I read the obituaries, sometimes the anniversary notices." Her shoulders gave a tiny shrug. "I just like to read about people and the lives they had together."

My throat tightened, and I busied myself with the laminated menu, pretending to be intrigued by so many choices. I wondered what my mother thought about her own life. What would she change? What moments would she live over and over again? Did she wonder at how even through all the pain, it had still been beautiful and gone by so fast? What would she want the paper to say about her life, for the world to read about over breakfast with their daughters? Tears burned my eyes as I thought about how empty her life would sound, eighty-four years of living crushed into a two-inch column. No one reading it would understand what her life had been. That would be left up to me alone. But even I didn't know a goddamn thing.

Before my nose formed the lopsided bump of physical proof, I had tortured myself with conspiracy theories. In 1964, the year I was born, no one had babies past the age of forty. My parents had been married sixteen years before I came along, and yet I had no siblings. Something had to be off, I was sure of it.

"Am I really your daughter?" I asked my mother when I was twelve, as I leaned over the kitchen counter that still held the faded stain of her blood.

My mother had looked into my face and smiled, a real smile, and her voice almost purred, filled with a fleeting wholeness, as she reached out to stroke my cheek. "You're all mine, baby girl. All mine."

———

But if I am yours, then you are mine. What happens when you are gone?

Science Dork? Science Dork, I lived inside her shell. What is the name of the strands that attached me to her? I floated warm and happy inside a womb percolating with anxiety, then she labored to push me out into a world I learned to fight and fear. I was once inside her, but now she's inside me.

———

"Kate?" My mother's voice is a croak.

I lean over her. "Yes?"

"Turn off the TV."

I click the remote and the picture dissolves. In the darkness of the screen, my reflection appears, filmy and ghostlike, but I can still make out our nose. The silence bears down like a weight on my chest, like it is my lungs that are failing.

"Mom?" I whisper.

But she is already asleep.

———

THE MAN ON THE SIDEWALK
BELONGS TO ME

I jog past him at sunrise, desperate to calm a mind clicking with chatter.

He sits perched on a filthy duffel beneath the flimsy shelter of a jacaranda tree, its branches bending in the breeze, flinging purple blossoms, throwing itself away to gray streets of hardship, where only a slab of sidewalk bears our weight, where we crawl and crawl only to wind up back where we started.

His skin is weathered, wrinkled, brown. Silently he smokes and sips from a 40 ounce silver bullet, wearing clothes the shade of concrete, a clever camouflage. People like me rush past, ignoring him, occupied with careless lives, stopping only to stare at tiny screens, blissfully unaware we know almost nothing about the world.

My mind whirrs, moving too fast, complicating everything in its solicitude. What did he possess before his loss? If he sits on my side of the property line does he belong to me? Do I own the crows cawing in the sky? These are pointless questions and I abandon them like thousands others.

The light fades. It starts to rain. Purple petals stir in the wind, spinning in a reckless dance of color then falling to rest on the ground. The air starts to smell like the jacaranda blossoms, silky blooms littering the sidewalk, beautiful trash to be swept away, discarded.

VISITOR

I set up shop on the road across from the women's prison, because that seems as good a place as any. I have two boxes of counterfeit Ray-Bans to sell, men's, women's and children's sizes, all lifted from the Sunglass Haven where I work, and now have to come home with enough cash to make rent.

I set up my table, organize inventory into rows of Wayfarers, Aviators, Jackie Ohhs, and sit down in my folding chair to wait. I stare at the expanse of sky, the long empty road, pretending I've crossed some distant border. Two hours pass but no one comes.

Finally in the distance a ball of dust streams toward me and I watch, waiting for it to morph into the shape of a car. It stops in front of me and a tall lean man steps out, sauntering toward me like Clint Eastwood in *Dirty Harry*. A little blonde girl trails after him, wearing what appears to be a shiner, three days old by the looks of it. The man catches me staring.

"Bumped right into the edge of the kitchen table and that's what happened. Can you believe it?"

I look into his eyes, icy blue and full of venom, leveled on me like a warning.

"Ought to sue the landlord or whoever makes that goddamn table," he says, lighting a Marlboro. Then he holds the match like someone at a stadium concert, letting a hint of breeze extinguish it.

"She's been so embarrassed 'bout it too." The man shrugs, drags on his cigarette. "I don't know why. She's only five and like they say, 'stuff happens.'" He drops the cigarette and crushes it with his heel, then rests his icy stare back on me. "Lucky we came about you, in't it? Imagine that. Sunglasses for sale. All the way out here."

The girl reaches for a miniature set of neon pink shades and I kneel before her to help, gently resting the frames on the bridge of her tiny nose. I feel her breath on my face, light and cool, smelling like bubblegum and innocence. It's eighty degrees out but a chill runs through me, followed by that feeling when you walk through a spider web, something invisible but insistent tangling across my skin. I hold a mirror so she can see herself and a smile seeps across her face. I let my fingers stroke the length of her cheek as I pull away.

"How much?" says the man, reaching into his pocket.

"Ten."

He fishes out a bill and hands it to me, then turns toward the car. "Let's go, Squirt. Time to see mama."

I don't want them to go and fumble stupidly for more time, as if another minute with this girl might convince me her life will turn out okay. "You need a pair, mister?"

He levels those eyes on me again and I crumple beneath his gaze. He slides inside the front seat without a word, the girl following.

I watch them turn left and disappear behind barriers at the prison entrance, trailing billows of dust that eclipse the sky, leaving me at the side of the road, alone again, thinking of everything but rent.

———

IN DEFENSE OF MEMORY LOSS

"Eggs," my mother snaps. "Eggs, damn it. I had eggs for breakfast."

But she didn't. Just like she didn't ride the bus downtown this morning, didn't get a black eye from her father, and didn't steal lemons from the neighbor's yard.

She strains when I ask questions, staring into the blank wall in front of us as if paint and drywall hold the answers. She slumps in her chair, head covered in white wisps of frizz, looking like a cat who has been beat badly, over-matched in a long fight, retreating to nurse and lick the wounds of a lifetime.

She has questions too. *Where am I? When can I go home?* Questions for which I have no answer. On the shelf are photos that haunt me, visions of my younger self. In each one I pose on the paisley couch where my mother and I spent evenings watching *The Rockford Files, Police Woman, Quincy, M.E.*, the same couch where I sat stiff and insistent, saying I had no idea how those clove cigarettes had wound up in my jacket, the couch where years later Blair Watson sweet-talked me out of my Calvin Kleins, fingers stalking my pale inner thigh. My mother hated Blair, detested every man I ever dated. In college, she'd gone apoplectic after learning I was dating a bass player. "A *musician?*" she scoffed. "Good goddamn luck. They string you along. Then, when it's too late, you see it's just another show. But you've already been emptied. You've been gutted like a goddamn fish."

She recalls none of this. She knows my face, knows I married a man with a toupee and that I have a cat who once bit her, but she doesn't know my age, or where I work, or that I can't sleep at night. She doesn't know she spent twenty years working as a hotel maid, her responsibility in each room to erase all evidence that anyone else had ever existed there.

There are things we inherit from our mothers. I won't inherit a diamond ring or strand of pearls. Mine has already given me everything she once possessed, a tin box filled with recipes written on index cards, a photo album, a face, a strangling fear of the world.

Here and there, mother. Now and then. A gathering of moments you have folded and tucked away into the past tense.

———

SEEING

We walk the same streets as another restless day tapers off, anxiety pumping through each limb as we pass the sleeping homeless, silently remembering how our mother dressed us as bums one Halloween because she'd prepared no other costume, how she recast us into smudge-faced little ragamuffins, but now these bodies around us are grotesque carcasses we won't step near for fear they will reach out, infect us with their loss, their sorrowful stench, transforming us with a touch into them . . . and as we hurry past I try to distract you by pointing to the trees, their branches riding on the breeze, licking at the sky and I show you what I see inside their shapes, a woman shaking a cane like a threat, a weeping long nosed dog, a monocled bear, but when I try to make you see what I see, your eyes fade, you won't look at my trees and I feel your heart return to its crypt as you stare down the gray concrete under our feet, saying, your voice a low warning, hand gripping mine, nails digging into my flesh, that visions like mine only appear in clouds.

—

HOW TO READ YOUR FATHER'S
OBITUARY

Read, through eyes flat as a rag doll's, "Sam Dwyre. Born San Francisco December 15, 1927. Died San Francisco January 16, 2009. Career civil servant." Read behind closed doors. Under no circumstances should you read in public. This means train, bus, or any other mode of public transportation and includes the reception area of the law firm where you answer phones because you can't find anything better right now.

Don't worry that the staccato bursts of words read like your father was cut from a piece of cardboard, a flimsy man with hollow insides. Don't bristle when the words fail to capture the cadence of his laugh, the laugh you heard whenever he made his puns about pee, like the one about the tea-drinking Indian who drowned in his own Teepee, or the one he said every time you had peas for dinner, "Eat every carrot and pee on your plate!" You didn't get that joke for almost a year, and always wondered why he was being such a grouch when you were a good eater and didn't need such imperatives.

Feel no bitterness that the editors didn't give him the big half-page obit. Everyone knows those are paid for. But still, don't read any of those story tale life advertisements appearing on the same page with your father's lapidary obit. That will just make you feel worse.

Take no offense when it seems his life counts less because he is measured only by how many survivors he left behind: one daughter, whereas the guy in ıe next column had four brothers, three daughters, and fourteen grandchildren. This is just how they do it.

Do not feel guilty when under "Services" it reads simply, "None." This may sound like you are a selfish daughter who can't be bothered to honor the life of the man you have known every minute you've been alive, the man you cannot imagine living without. Sure, it reads a little cold, but remind yourself he didn't want formal services and in a couple of months when you can (hopefully) speak his name in more than a squeak, you are going to make a few calls and have a wake at The Blarney Stone where you will toast him with Guinness. You will raise your glass and share all your private moments, like the time you hadn't finished your book report and it was Sunday night, and your report was due Monday and you hadn't even finished Chapter One and you couldn't get further because it was *Treasure Island*, and you didn't know it then but even in your rambling hysteria you made a cogent argument about how it was gender bias for the school to even make you read this fucking book, and you were panicked and he told you he would be right back and you were like, "You're leaving? Now???" and you seethed with the betrayal, stunned that YOUR OWN FATHER could leave you at a time like this, and you threw yourself on your pink bedspread and sobbed and then he came back forty minutes later, standing over you holding something called *Cliff Notes*.

Do not think in metaphors. Like how he is already starting to fade, his life as soundless as your footsteps on the carpet beside his bed. Or how it's like you were playing happily on a see-saw together but he hopped off his end without warning, sending you down to hit the ground with a thud.

Do not ponder the meaning of obituaries. Don't wonder, if news of his death is printed but no one reads it and no one ever knows –is he really gone? Philosophical musings won't help you now.

If someone catches you and asks, "Whatcha readin'?" tell them to mind their own fucking business.

Throw the paper away immediately. Crumple it in a loud, passive-aggressive ball. (Remember to recycle).

Prepare for the year of firsts. The first Christmas, your first birthday without him. Learn to live in a world that does not have him in it.

Do not recall his last weeks, when all you did was nag him to eat better and get his hearing checked. And do not recall his last days, especially not the day you forced him to go to the hospital and he looked at you through eyes puddled with tears and told you he didn't want to go, and when you asked why not he said, "Because I'm afraid I won't come back this time." Do not think about that.

Make mistakes at work. Transpose phone numbers on messages and when people complain, shrug and give them your best glassy-eyed stare, saying, "That's the number they gave me."

Realize, slowly, that nothing will ever feel right again.

Leave work early. Resist the urge to drive by the house where you grew up, the wide bungalow where your father lived for forty-four years, the home he refused to leave unless it was "Feet first!" That place no longer exists and if you turn back to look at it now, you could turn to stone, like what happened to Lot's wife, and no one likes turning to stone.

Go home. Watch the president's inaugural address on TV, even though your father was a Hillary supporter. Cry during the part about what so many Americans have lost. When your friend touches your arm and asks in her most tender voice, "What's wrong?" Sob and tell her, "It's just so sad." "What's sad?" she'll say. Yank your arm back and yell, "The poems! All the lost poems!" When she squeezes your hand and tells you softly, "Honey, he said *homes*. All the lost *homes*," decide it's time to get your own hearing checked.

———

ALL THE BAD WORDS START WITH V

Every night when I called my mother she asked the same question, "What are you making Mark for dinner?" though she knew I worked twelve hour days and didn't cook. Rather than absorbing the startled, "Oh?" if I said, "Nothing Mom, we'll probably just order pizza," I began to lie, making up elaborate menus. Grilled lamb chops with organic white corn and crispy roast potatoes. Blackened tilapia smothered in black bean mango salsa. Pan seared halibut with heirloom tomatoes on a bed of Moroccan couscous. I felt guilty for lying to my mother, but once I had started, I couldn't stop. Lying is contagious.

Eight months ago, Mark and I rushed out the door, late for my boss Gwen's wedding. Rummaging for my sunglasses in the glove compartment of Mark's Land Rover, my hand grasped a small plastic bottle of baby oil.

"What's this?" I asked, holding it up. Mark and I do not have a baby.

"Oh, that." Mark gripped the steering wheel as his right eyebrow twitched. "I needed change for a parking meter, so I ran in to Rite-Aid and bought that."

I stared at my husband of nine years and waited for the rest of the explanation, the part that made sense, but he just gazed straight ahead, fixated on the road.

I frowned and thought about what Mark said. I'd needed change before. I had run inside a drugstore, purchased gum, water, Diet Coke –anything close to the register. I never once ventured into the fluorescent depths of Aisle 9A, Baby Needs/Cleaning Supplies.

"Why didn't you just buy a pack of gum?"

"What?" Mark glanced in my direction and I swore I saw the whites of his eyes. "I don't chew gum. You know that. I thought you could use it. For your bath, you know."

It was true that in nine years I had never seen Mark chew gum. And I did use baby oil in my baths. Praying to smooth out dryness, wrinkles, and the crepey skin I saw sagging around my forty-four-year-old neck every time I looked in the mirror.

Fingering the generic label on the bottle, there was no question that my husband had purchased this. Anyone else might have sprung for Johnson & Johnson. Not Mark, a painfully frugal man.

I twisted open the pink cap. The silver protective foil had been pierced. I studied the oil level in the bottle.

"Why is it open?" I asked.

No answer.

"Mark! Why is it open?" I heard my voice, high, screechy and far away, like it had come from someone else.

"Jesus Christ! I used some for the patch of dry skin on my elbow. Get off my fucking back, okay?"

Holding the gift that my considerate husband had thought to purchase but forgotten to give me, I considered. I could conduct a national survey of 20,000 men and women, a sampling encompassing every age, race, religion, educational level and socio-economic status. Not one of them would believe this bullshit story.

I would not let him off the hook. I would do what Gwen, my boss and best friend in the Sex Crimes Unit of the District Attorney's office, had trained me to do: ask crafted questions, questions for which there were no misunderstandings, no lies by omission, no outs. I would keep going until I hit pay dirt.

First the open-ended inquiry, an interrogation designed to elicit information: List all possible uses for baby oil. (I ran through this list mentally: babies, baths, skin moisturizer, tanning, jerking off, sexual lubricant.) Did you fuck someone? (past tense) Are you fucking someone? (present tense)

Did you pick up a hooker? Beat off in your car? Why in God's name is this in your car??!

Next came cross-examination. Questions to afford maximum control, something I needed because my hands had started to shake. A quiz for the slippery witness who would lie through his teeth unless boxed in: We do not have a baby, correct? You failed to actually bring this purported gift to me, correct? You have not touched me in six weeks, correct? These questions had only one answer and allowed the questioner to escort the witness right into her trap, where he would give it all up, everything the inquisitor needed to . . . to what?

But I posed none of these queries. Instead I listened to his story in my mind, hitting rewind and play over and over again. It's possible, I told myself. It could maybe be true. I closed my eyes and imagined our early years, before the tight forced smiles and restless sighs. I saw Mark in my old apartment gripping daisies, their heads leaning sideways on their stems. We lived three hundred miles apart then and it was the end of our first weekend together, a weekend spent with the curtains drawn, keeping the speed of our bodies lithe and slow. His green eyes had puddled with worry as he asked, "What happens when weekends aren't enough?"

I sat through Gwen's wedding and tried not to cringe during the vows.

———

In the weeks that followed, I tried to ignore the baby oil that haunted me. Hunching over the coffee table eating dinner with Mark, I studied his chiseled profile, stared at his gigantic schnazz and wondered if it had grown a tiny bit longer, like Pinocchio's. Mark burned his mouth on the pizza and inside I laughed. Some cultures punish liars by cutting out their tongues. But is it the tongue that lies, or the heart?

Mark snapped on the TV and clicked through dozens of channels before landing on *Fatal Attraction*. I couldn't stop from narrating. "How could Michael Douglas want a crazy skank like that when he has such a beautiful wife?...This is where Michael Douglas realizes he ruined his whole life for two nights of pussy... This is where Michael Douglas gets what's coming to him." Then Mark chimed in through a mouthful of pepperoni, "And to think he could have avoided all of it with a $4 box of condoms."

I winced and stood up to take my plate to the sink.

———

Mark started coming home later and later. Showing condos to new buyers who work late, he explained. He wasn't hungry, didn't want a drink. Trying to cut down, he said, lose this gut. He slapped and gripped a nonexistent belly and I wondered whether those on the receiving end were responsible for their own deception.

———

The next Saturday, Mark neglected to turn off his computer before leaving to show an over-priced two-bedroom craftsman to a pair of doe-eyed newly-weds. Telling myself it was okay to break the rules to learn if someone else was breaking the rules, I rushed through a split second of guilt as desperation trampled ideals. My stomach clenched and I thought of Bluebeard's wives as I held my breath and my hand curved over the mouse. Sifting through Mark's email, I noticed a lot of messages from someone named Tiffany, a "Junior Loan Officer" with Raymond Flatt Capital, the mortgage brokerage that shared space with Mark's real estate office. I clicked through the screens on a frenetic mission to know.

Some messages prickled my skin:

May 6, 8:36 a.m. "Good morning!! ☺"

May 7, 10:07 a.m. "Want to walk over to Starbucks? I'm going and would really love your company. Tiff"

My stomach fluttered a warning, creeping up from my gut to my throat, threatening to strangle me unless I stopped reading, but I clicked on, reading faster and faster, the words blurring but their message clear.

June 3, 1:12 p.m., "You need to come have a drink with me later." 1:13 p.m., Mark's reply, "Yeah, baby!"

June 6, 5:40 p.m., "What time are we going to dinner? Xoxoxoxo Tiff."

I ransacked Mark's desk, found the June 6th receipt for $120 in wine and sushi, recalled the conflicting story about who he was with, why he was so late, why he stood me up for our weekly date to watch *Breaking Bad*.

And then, the detonation:

June 12, 3:16 p.m., Mark's email to Tiff, "Meet me at 510 Washington Street?" 3:18 p.m., her reply, ". . .Only if you play Enigma. . ." Then his email two hours later, "I can't even think straight after that. Holy cow. . ." And her reply, "xoxoxoxoox."

I Googled Enigma, hoping against hope it was a video game, but discovered a band whose "sultry, sexy new release, *Principles of Lust*, ignites stark sensuality, taking the listener on a breathy journey of passion." The slow certainty of pain stabbed my stomach and I ran to the bathroom and vomited in the sink.

"It's sex music," Gwen said matter of factly when she could finally understand the words I choked into the phone. "You need to find out whether 510 Washington is vacant."

I already knew that it was and sobbed harder. "Christ, I feel so stupid. I'm such a cliché. Such a fucking. . .victim."

"Did you ever notice how all the really bad words start with 'V'?" Gwen asked.

"No."

"They do. Victim. Vile. Vermin—"

"Viper, venereal, vitiate. . .Vows." The word stung my tongue.

Gwen's voice softened. "Are you gonna be okay?"

"Yeah." I blew my nose and hung up the phone. I wasn't okay. I wasn't okay at all.

In their fit of heartbreak and rage, most people cut their spouse's face out of their photos. But I cut out my own image in every snapshot except the crystal-framed wedding photo propped on the nightstand next to our bed. I tore that one from behind its glass, pulled out a black sharpie and captioned my smiling face, "*Stupid trusting bitch.*"

———

I confronted Mark in a tearful frenzy without enough evidence to convict. His forked tongue flickered as he lied his face off and because of my strategic error and tight-stretched hope, I had no choice but to take it.

"That dinner wasn't a date. It was a meeting. She was giving me the name of a business contact . . . She had to visually inspect the Washington property for the bank to approve the loan…I didn't lie, okay? I just omitted some things . . . Enigma? I don't even know what she was talking about . . . Okay, maybe I flirted. Maybe I pushed the envelope in some emails. But nothing happened, I swear . . . She's not my type, anyway. Six feet tall and big." He emphasized *big*. "With great big man hands. *Bleeachk!*" Mark made the same face he made once after chugging from a carton of sour milk, and tacked on a shudder to prove his disgust.

———

My brain hissed and whirred, reciting the emails, the explanations, the missing fragments, imagining all that it didn't know. Could Mark be telling the truth? I thought back to a time when Mark meant every word he said, and I tried to believe. I did believe, until the facts flew back up and smacked my face. There was a voice. A Voice that screamed me awake at 3 a.m. No, dummy, it said. *No.* Days passed and The Voice got louder, chronicling my displaced life with a question mark at the end of each observation. You're still here? *Really?* The Voice shored up my new existence, doubting every step, mocking me through my sweat soaked insomnia. It spun me in circles tighter, faster, until I didn't know what was real. I couldn't deny this thing Mark had dumped in my lap, and couldn't leave it alone. With the mangled wreckage of a serenity prayer, I struggled to know for sure. If I really knew what happened, I'd know what to do.

Masochistic in my determination to fill in the missing pieces, pieces of me flew away. Everywhere I looked, on the street, at the beach, in restaurants, I saw Mark's lovers. The ghosts of Betrayal Past, Betrayal Present and Betrayal Future were tall, short, slender, curvy, busty, athletic, blue-eyed, beautiful and never, never me. Every woman loomed as a foe. The black haired girl at California Coffee Roasters who flashed a toothy smile at Mark as he asked for a bone dry cappuccino and then still smiling, forgot to take my order. The blonde up the street wearing short shorts that rode up her ass as she swung it back and forth walking Bosco, her chocolate lab, lingering to flirt with Mark as he pulled weeds in our front yard. The Voice got louder. He'd fuck *her*, it said. Then my head swiveled to glance up the block toward a leggy red head. He'd *definitely* fuck her, screamed The Voice. Over and over, day after frantic day, until I couldn't hear the sound of my own breath.

———

Gwen once slashed the tires of her then-fiancé's Mercedes with a bowie knife she had borrowed from the evidence locker. He had exchanged too many pleasantries with a big-titted waitress who served them rib-eyes and spinach salads at Ruth's Chris Steakhouse. I was no tire-slasher, certainly no stalker—and yet found my car steering its way to Bay Side Realty. I was no longer myself.

I pulled into the garage, sliding into a Raymond Flatt Capital parking space that warned, "Clients Only. All Others Will Be Towed." Snapping off the engine, I sat still in the cool darkness, listening to a staccato heartbeat pound inside my ears. I teetered in the front door and walked queasy laps around the office, pretending to look for Mark, playing the loving wife stopping by to say hello, really searching in vain for the promised fat chick.

Through glass walls, my eyes landed on a five-foot-seven shimmering blonde with delicate, manicured hands. The nameplate on her desk read, "Tiffany Dandridge" and a yellow smiley face stuck to its edge. I hid around the corner, staring at her ass, the circumference of her arms, hoping I was going blind, praying for a layer of lard to appear on Tiff Smiley-Face's petite frame so I could sleep again, so I could believe my husband wasn't a liar after all, but the only part of her that was big were those breasts.

"May I help you?" I jumped and turned to peer into the face of an agent I had never seen before.

"I – I – I was just looking for the restroom."

He pointed down the hall and I quivered a smile of thanks.

Tiff's tight black pencil skirt hypnotized me. It was identical to the skirt I had worn the first night Mark's hand ever grazed my thigh, making the tiny soft blonde hairs stand on end. The Tiffster tossed her long shiny hair, sat down and picked up the phone, spoke and smiled into the receiver, hung up, stood up, and marched in my direction. My adrenalin surged and dizzy panic took over. What to do? I'll say hi. Introduce myself. No, I'll confront her. Tackle her. NO. I'll flee.

I bolted for the door, escaping into the cave of the garage. My face crumpled and I settled into my car and let the tears pour. I had longed to find a shriveled hag with warts on her face, maybe even a hunchback. But Tiff was pretty. Undeniably pretty.

Mark sighed when I confronted him with the evidence of Tiffany's petite stature. "Listen, Allie. If we can't even agree on whether a woman is overweight, then we've got a real problem." He squeezed my stupid, trusting shoulder and apologized for crossing the line with some emails. I looked at him with my stupid trusting eyes and said, "Are you fucking kidding me?" but not out loud.

"Next time, pull your evidence together before you go after him," Gwen warned when I called.

And so I thought about next time. All I thought about was next time.

———

Gwen gave me two weeks off to pull myself together. Shattered, needy, still desperate for more clues, I used the time to rifle through Mark's suit pockets, sniff his shirts, study his credit card statements. I shivered on the couch alone, crying so hard I worried about dehydration, watching the clock, waiting like a high strung puppy for Mark to walk through the door.

Mark acted surprised when I asked where he had been. "I still need to work, don't I?" he whined, "People want to go see property after work. Sometimes I'll be late. You've got to get over it."

I got over it by mutating into a cartoon character flattened by a train, a thin pancake of my former self. Nothing looked the same and I waited to feel firm ground again, but it didn't come and I plunged backwards, weightless. I went to a shrink, who suggested medication, and that seemed unfair somehow. Pausing over the prescription pad at the close of our session, the doctor stared at me and asked, "Can you rebuild the trust?"

I knew what she really meant was, "Can you stop picking the scab?" But I didn't think I could, no matter how much they medicated me. Deep or shallow, the wound was there. I might as well feel it.

Back home alone on the couch again, I channel surfed, trying to land on a happy movie, a show with a laugh track. I tried not to think, tried to halt the images of the unspoken invitation preceding, "Only if you play Enigma…" but I couldn't catch a break. Clicking through the stations, I found *Working Girl*, but reeled when Alec Baldwin got caught popping Doreen DiMucci. On *Sex And The City*, Carrie pressed at her tear ducts, confessing to Aiden that she had fucked Big. Even on CNN, John Edwards swelled with contrition as he admitted to a long time affair.

———

The meds sent me back to earth with a thud and the sickness of doubt, of hoping but not believing, wrenched itself into the searing realization that Mark was all I wanted, that losing him meant losing everything. A new strain of panic set in as I peered down at my baggie flannels, the chipped polish on my toes, and my audition began. I plucked the hoary pubic hair, shopped for lacy underwear that rode up *my* ass, discovered that just showed off a lot of cellulite, joined the gym, worked out, stopped eating, hit the tanning bed, feigned an interest in leaving the house. Oh, pick *me*! cried The Voice. On the treadmill, my brain kept at its mission, replaying the events, still begging with each pounding step to know. But running in place, going nowhere fast, a glimmer of a new thought flickered behind The Voice. Something about my tryout seemed off kilter –backwards even, like words reversed in a mirror:

!!! SDNE EVOL

———

Now two months have passed since I found the emails. It's another Saturday and Mark and I are at our first gay wedding. Jeff, an agent in Mark's office, is marrying his long time partner, Trevor. The thought of sitting through a wedding seems unbearable, a feeling fueled perhaps by the percolating anxiety that Tiffany might be among the guests. I fidget in my new Gucci dress that I can't afford but which seemed like a necessity. Craning my neck to scan the church, I'm relieved that WhoreFace is not seated among the shiny gorgeous gay men stuffed into the pews.

The vows begin promptly and Jeff goes first. "Trevor, you are my best friend and I love you so much. I am prepared for the challenges that being married to you will involve." The church erupts into laughter and Jeff has to pause before continuing. Why do we find it so comical when a simple truth gets spoken out loud? "I promise to be fully present in the time that we share together, to love and enjoy you, to support you in your goals, to share myself fully while we share our lives."

Within minutes, the vows are over and no one has guaranteed love until death, no one has pledged to always be faithful, no one has sworn togetherness forever, No Matter What. No one has denied that it takes two to love or made promises they cannot possibly keep. I unclench my hands as I realize no one has lied.

———

After the wedding, I call my mother at 7:30, just like every other night. She knows nothing of my marital tsunami. I tell her nothing because I can't bear to speak the words out loud, to think about how the words would sound inside her ears.

Right on cue tonight she asks, "What are you making Mark for dinner?"

I take a breath before answering and in this moment decide. It's time to stop telling lies. Even if it's only to myself.

CONTRADICTION

Lodged in that space between dreaming and waking, a shrill noise ripples inside my ears. The sound rises, gathers shape, and I recognize the ring of a phone. It's New Year's morning and I've barely slept.

"Come get me," you say. Not a question but a demand.

"Where?" I ask, even though I already know.

Driving, I count out loud. 2009 – *one*. 2010 – *plus three*. 2013 – *plus one*. When a person reaches five, even when events are broken up by time, that person goes to jail and stays for awhile.

Counting, I remember another New Year's – 1973. Running around the backyard, we banged pots and pans, shrieking *Happy New Year!* when all we were happy about was that no one was forcing us to go to bed. We didn't know yet about the need for fresh starts.

The next morning our mother sat cloaked in a blue silk robe, stirring cold coffee. Her fists clenched. Every breath was a sigh. A hummingbird buzzed at our empty feeder, trying for success again and again. We couldn't name it but somehow knew an empty feeder meant cruel neglect. Our mother's eyes lifted from her coffee to the tiny bird. "Bastard," she said. This was what she said when our stepfather hadn't come home. This was our cue to slip outside.

We wanted breakfast. We wanted to sit in our pajamas and watch *I Love Lucy*. But instead we flew around the backyard, hummingbirds ourselves, acting out dramas, pretending to be Cowboys & Indians, Cops & Robbers, anything where you got to chase me with a weapon and fierce eyes. *"Bastard!"* you yelled. *"Bastard!"* I screamed back, giggling. In our games, we recited our mother's lines. We sang out, "You are *such* a disappointment." Then we cocked our plastic guns and said *Pow*.

You pulled out a crumpled dollar, smoothed it flat on your blue-jeaned thigh and read aloud like you had found a poem in your pocket, "In God We Trust." We grinned at this stupidity. Our only faith in this wrinkled paper was its promise to deliver two donuts and a chocolate milk. You told me to search my pockets and I did, knowing already they were empty. "That's okay," you assured me.

Donut Star was closed. We stared through the storefront windows disbelieving our betrayal but couldn't see inside. All we could see was our reflection.

"Is that really what I look like?" you asked. I felt you vibrating before the glass studying your reflection and knew you were thinking, *I love this boy. I hate this boy.*

When I pick you up after a DUI you have the same pissed-on garbage smell, the fragrance of despair. I steer us to Krispy Kreme but the gleaming doors are locked. A sign in the window says, Closed for New Year's Day. I look at you, then we laugh until we cry. Through wet eyes I see you, a hummingbird flying toward the glass. You won't see your reflection until it's too late.

———

SARA TURNER'S SUBLIME TIMELINE

OF GRIEF

[November 16, 1975]

For no good reason, we hate her.

Maybe it's the spackles of freckles covering every inch of her wide flat face, hair the color of dishwater, eyes like mud. Or because she is big --five feet six, legs like tree trunks and a belly of blubber. Unlike us, she has tits, but the flabby kind that sprout from a diet of pure starch. Her clothes are sometimes dirty and she smells like yeast.

"We know you're poor, but how much does it cost to buy a bar of soap?" Julie is the one who sneers rhetorical questions. The rest of us are less imaginative in our cruelty, taunting uninspired insults and calling her "Fat Sara."

Avenging nothing, we form a circle and kick at her shins. Sweat darkens Fat Sara's armpits and we smell the scent of her fear. It fuels us, arousing something primal. The monster inside me comes alive. I am finally more than a wispy twelve year old girl. I am finally enormous, dangerous, capable of causing misery. There is vast guilty comfort in knowing I can reduce someone to ruins.

Fat Sara tries to pretend it's all in good fun. "Come on you guys—" The words spill like feathers from her mouth.

We mimic her in a dozen different voices, each sharp as a needle.

"Come on you guys."

"Come on you guys!"

"COME ON YOU GUYS!" Julie growls the deepest, a satanic sotto voce. Then she turns, sticks her ass in the air and farts in Sara's direction.

[*January 27, 1976*]

She is under our spell. American voodoo where the pack of Chihuahuas wearing fuzzy pink sweaters and long leashes lunge at the German Shepherd because they are spoiled and rash and don't know they're small. We chase Sara around the slippery classroom floor, cornering her on the losing side of a hexagon of desks. There are three of us, one of her, and still Sara could kick our skinny asses if the thought would ever cross her mind.

Watching someone fall is a hilarious event to witness, but it becomes wickedly delicious when you know you are the cause. How time stands still while a body flies, suspended in air as if by magic, until gravity asserts itself and a head connects with furniture. The expression on the person's face is priceless.

"She fell!" we laugh, "Fat Sara fell!"

Sara wipes blood from her mouth and her chin quivers as she tries not to cry.

Somewhere deep inside I celebrate how straightforward torture is, how profanely candid.

[*March 15, 1976*]

She tries to pretend she's invisible.

"FUCK YOU," we call out. *FUCK YOU* we gouge into her desk, delighted to inflict permanent damage into something so hard.

We steal her purse, jumping on it until we hear something inside go *Crack*, swinging it in circles above our heads until it's like the blades of a helicopter. We let go and watch our very first physics lesson explode across a tree. It detonates lunch money, hair brush, Kotex. I feel a tingle of pleasure as we obliterate pieces of Sara.

"Viral little bitches," Mr. Rady says, returning from the teacher's lounge reeking of Winstons. We don't know what viral means but we like the sound of it.

When Sara finally tattles, Mr. Rady does nothing, enlisting as silent conspirator in our sweet game of pain.

[*June 14, 1976*]

On the last day of school, Fat Sara stands next to the flag pole. A piss yellow Maverick pulls up, belching black smoke from its exhaust. In the backseat are clear plastic bags loaded with hundreds of empty cans, aluminum carcasses Sara and her family will trade for a few dollar bills and coins inscribed *In God We Trust.* A man with a face the color of concrete leans over and opens the passenger door. Sara slips in silently, looking straight ahead and disappears from my life forever.

[*Today. Now. Always.*]

Shadows of Fat Sara still inhabit my existence after so many years. I picture myself then. Still a child. Almost innocent. Not yet haunted by flaws, not yet knowing enough to fear what I would become. Are all children so adept at torture? Do we prey on each other to abate the fear inside us? Only now can I comprehend the lesson Sara and I taught one another: that life would be pointlessly cruel and seeped in regret. I imagine her patience in showing up at school each day, hoping, all evidence to the contrary, that life might get better. Now I am Sara. No one can save me. I can't seem to save myself.

———

TELLING TIME

The day our stepmother Ruthie served us meatloaf sandwiches for lunch, you took a bite and pretended to gag.

"Tastes like monkey shit on drywall," you said, crumbs flying from your lips.

Ruthie stepped back toward us, slid the plate from the table and dumped it on your head. Then she walked to her bedroom and went to sleep. She had stopped trying to pretend we belonged to her.

We rinsed gravy from your hair, splashing each other at the kitchen sink, then drifted outside, squinting in the sun, hearts yearning for the soothing boredom of routine. Somewhere deep inside we wondered: What if it doesn't get better than this? We were so busy yearning we couldn't hear the music of the birds.

⸺

I wanted a sister. To appease me you sat still, letting me roll your long soft hair in pink sponge curlers while you taught me how to tell time.

"The big hand will always kick the little hand's ass in the contest of movement." You reached over your shoulder to give me another curler, then pointed at the clock on the kitchen wall. "Minutes jump by first, then the hours. Don't forget that."

I promised I wouldn't.

Time passed that day just like you said it would and we fell asleep, only to be startled awake.

"You little queer!" Ruthie's voice was a screech when she saw you. Only the sponge of my rollers saved your head from her slaps.

———

In a neighborhood where police helicopters buzz low overhead I find you drooping in one of the bars you haunt. When I tell you Ruthie has died you don't flinch or even blink, so I raise the topic of meatloaf and curlers. You say my memory is flawed. This is what you say after going off the meds.

"You make up stories," you slur. "They're whispered by an insomniac wind. In the history of time, your heart is too loud." Eyes smoldering, you swat at a black fly hovering over the bar.

"In these lies you make up, everyone lives but no one survives." You swat again at the fly, though it has already disappeared. "You are my paper mâché sister. I made you what you are."

The hands on the clock move so fast they make me dizzy.

———

SWOON

When our eyes first meet, me stepping through an entryway glowing in the light of a bulb caged in a hexagon of blood red glass, you still in the blackness of the street, you are just a man.

When your body throws its shadow onto the threshold where I stand, I turn, stare, size you up, file you into a category, disposing of you. *Grad student, squinty eyes, social prospects thin as his pale hair.* You have catalogued me too. *Foolish, vain, impatient enough to walk home alone in empty darkness.*

I turn my back on you, a person of no significance, finishing my path home. When your footsteps follow, moving into the garish glow of my hallway, they echo the promise that you will prove how much you matter.

The knife pulled from your pocket is so ordinary, so unassuming, a lot like you. You lunge and spin my body in an effortless dance, cupping your hand to my mouth, gripping the back of my body to yours, moving us both to the brink. I freeze, coiled in your embrace. We are layered in color. The salty taste of your skin on my mouth, your heaving breath beneath my back, the smell of your sweat, the scent of my fear. Together we breathe. We don't speak. There are no words. *Who has ever held me so close?* I wonder. I feel precious somehow. I think I might be your first.

But in our visceral pose, there is the matter of the ordinary knife at my throat. Choices must be made. Decisions one must make in any intimate relationship —*Where do we go from here?*

I inhale, absorbing the potency of your clutch, the scent of your intentions. I swoon, spiraling in a near perfect corkscrew twist, crashing onto cement.

I scream. After such a sound there can be nothing but silence and your footsteps fade in the distance. This is our beginning. For me, it will never end.

———

POSTCARDS IN *TEMPO RUBATO*

Dear Dr. No,

You spewed this word unbearably so many times it became your honorary title. Is it true that conflict avoidance is a key aspect of stress management during illness? *No.* Can you promise this will work? *No.* Do patients find Zoloft helps? *No.* Will weed kill the pain? *No.* Will I see Spring again? Your twitching smile was an abominable lie.

Dearest Love:

For years you trudged to court in sturdy shoes, wingtips that let you jump up crying, "*Objection!*" Those shoes cradled your feet as you walked from court to jail, visiting clients you couldn't spring, those guilty of the worst, of failing too many times, of being born poor. You forfeited opera singing for a paycheck and me, and now you've been robbed. You switched my steady metronome to *tempo rubato* and for that I thank you. I hope you can retrace your steps and collect all those pieces of yourself you left behind.

Dear Cancer,

All is measured by you. Everything is better or worse, bigger or smaller, more or less than you. You insist on looming everywhere, always the center of attention. Remember when my son Andrew was five and he wanted a scary costume for Halloween so he decided to dress up as you? But he didn't know what you looked like and tugged at the sleeve of my robe begging, "Mama, show me what cancer looks like."

Dear Breasts,

Miss you! Wish you were here...

Dear Andrew,

I forgive you for flipping me off when I turned my back at the news stand, the time that muscled man intervened, yelling at you, saying a son shouldn't disrespect his mother, but he didn't understand your anger, did he? He couldn't see the stark betrayal in my hollow cheeks. I read in a magazine that day that when a mother holds her infant she unconsciously transmits how she views the world. I hope I taught you well. Pretty soon, all your teeth will fall out but they'll grow back again. And this other thing is going to be like that, strange at first, but something that happens, one of those things you survive.

Dear Fingers,

You can stop shaking now.

Dear Mother,

Is it possible all those things you told me as a child are true? That bad things happen everywhere? (What was your purpose in telling me that? To make me hyper-vigilant? To reassure me I wasn't alone once those things inevitably occurred?) If I'd had a childhood I would have spent it shrieking through sprinklers, rubber sneakers hydroplaning down slopes of soaked grass, eating raspberry jello with my hands. Sometimes I don't understand your intentions.

Dear Freedom,

I'm so tired. This feels like crossing a bridge in darkness, stopping at the middle, jumping. My stomach lurches as I become weightless just before hitting the water below and as I'm submerged, everything becomes dark dreamy radiance and I realize my body has at last learned how to sleep underwater and I can finally, finally rest.

———

UNDER

Mother won't let me in the water. Actually, she lets me step in, just no deeper than ankles. If I push it, drift a few more inches, the salty wetness licking at my calves, she scrambles up from her towel, running and cupping hands around her mouth so I can hear her voice above the rhythm of the waves. "*Riptides!*"

The sun bounces off the water, dazzling in its brightness. I like the ocean because waves crash with unstoppable force, but no one jumps out of their skin in terror, even when they break like a falling wall on someone's head. It's a soothing sort of violence, and I wonder what it would be like to feel a source so enormous striking, then tugging at my body, its commotion swallowing me, taking all of me, making this body part of something infinite. I ponder this momentum while sitting at the edge of the shore writing my name in wet sand, surrendering to the raw white foam of the tide, its surge erasing all trace of me again and again.

———

I'm sunburned so badly I have to stay home from school. Mother didn't know about Solarcaine. The skin on my cheeks and nose has blistered and auntie and cousin come over to gawk. "Can we pop it?" cousin asks.

"Jesus!" mother says, pushing them out the door.

"There's a name for people like her," auntie whispers, but she doesn't say what it is.

I fret sometimes over all the words I don't know.

"Aloe vera!" auntie calls out before the front door slams shut and they disappear.

Mother curses them, curses the sun. She flicks her lighter until it catches, sucks hard on a filtered cigarette, exhales a cloud of smoke. She draws the curtains to ward off the light, or maybe just to teach it a lesson. Then she lies down in her dim bedroom, a damp washcloth spread across her eyes.

I stand in front of the mirror, pressing down on the blisters, watching the water bulge beneath my skin. I want them to pop, to drip down my face like tears. I can't do it myself so I will them to do it on their own. Then I sit alone on my bed, practicing hating myself.

But a piece of the room is shining. Mother missed a spot and a sliver of sunlight forces its way in. I stand inside it, feeling its warmth on my blistered skin. I open my eyes wide, daring it to blind me. From the bedroom mother starts to wail. Her voice is loud, larger than waves crashing, and the sound pulls me down, taking me under.

—

THINGS I TRY TO DO WELL

Winged beasts attack my garden. Tier cakes lean and crumble like ramshackle castles, while water ballet leaves me dizzy, breathless, willing to drown. My shuttlecock tangles in the net, and birds refuse to sit still for my voyeur's gaze. Bowling balls slide to the gutter as tenpins mock my hope. Golf is a cruel Sisyphean task.

I accidentally swallow the Half Cent Liberty Cap from my coin collection and the buttonhole stitch becomes my bête noire. Clouds conspire to congregate before my telescope, erasing the stars, then my banjo snaps its string.

My taxidermy teacher turns out to be Norman Bates and extreme couponing wins me glares from hordes of shoppers crowding in tangled lines. Stamp collecting morphs me into a hoarding magpie and in the craft store my body seeps with dread, the shelves filled with mirrors of my imperfections, reflecting so many ways I might fail.

With these tasks I use to pass the time I justify myself, because if I don't fill the hours, why do I exist? My only choice is to sit, choke down loneliness, be still inside myself for the long silent moments, and that is just something I have never done well.

UNDONE

The doctor asks if I'll agree to take some tests. Simple stuff —reflex, Rorschach, Minnesota Multiphasic Personality Inventory. I don't see the harm, so I say yes. But I start having second thoughts.

The State of California can lock you up for seventy-two hours if you're a danger to yourself. I hit hour fifty-one before I remember the state can also commit you to a mental hospital for a whole year. A judge decides this after a 3.2 minute hearing, so you can bet that judge stakes a lot on the intake doctor's report, a doctor who in my case keeps asking, "How does someone like you wind up here?" until I want to slap him.

I know I messed up pretty badly. I understand that now, but I'm fairly certain a year in here will only make things worse. And considering this past year and beyond, the things that led me here, I'm not so sure my life can be inventoried.

I open the test booklet anyway. If I have to, I'll use their tool. I'll play along and use their words to tell my story. They want a map to crazy? I'll show them crazy. I'll show them just how easy it all comes undone.

———

This personality inventory consists of random statements. Read each statement and decide whether it is true or false as applied to you. If a statement is true, blacken the bubble marked T on the sheet provided. If a statement is false, blacken the circle marked F. ONLY USE A NUMBER TWO PENCIL!!! A separate sheet is provided in the event you feel compelled to explain your answers.

1. I am friendly, even toward people doing things considered wrong.   --True

Last January, barely two years out of law school, I got promoted to felonies. No more misdemeanor domestic violence, petty theft, or traffic court. Now I represented rapists, drug dealers, child molesters, men who fucked their wives up good. I was on the way up.

"The whole point of being a lawyer is to handle bigger and better cases," my boss Henry said, giving me the news. In the L.A. Public Defender's Office, "bigger and better" meant clients facing decades in prison, maybe a third strike, and facts that curled your hair. My new stack of files included a vehicular manslaughter, possession for sale of twenty kilos of cocaine, and rape of an eighty-year-old woman at gunpoint. Each one was slated for trial one after the other.

I was in way over my head, but I loved Henry's attitude and crowded around to hear his stories at the bar where a party had been thrown together in my honor. Any defense lawyer was sick of getting cornered at parties and tortured with questions like, "How can you defend *those people*?" But unlike me, Henry had all the answers.

"My uncle once asked, 'How would you feel if you set a guilty man free with your fast talking?'" Henry swigged his beer, pausing before feeding his punch line. "I'd feel great! Putting a guilty man back on the street is the greatest testament to my skills as a trial lawyer."

We cheered and raised our glasses, but even though it was my big night, my laughter was forced. Pumped up on beers and bravado, it was all about ego, who was the best, who got away with something in court. Lawyers were like a pack of dogs who took comfort in one another. Together we were strong, alone weak. At home, in the darkness before sleep, we would all feel differently.

I snuck outside to call my Dad and tell him about my promotion.

"Honey that's wonderful," he said, "I'm so proud of you."

If my father had reservations about his only child's career choice, he kept them to himself. He might not always understand me, but his devotion had proven life's only certainty.

"How are you feeling?" I asked.

"I'm in pretty good shape," he coughed, "For the shape I'm in."

"I'll see you for dinner Sunday?"

"Sure thing, honey."

I hung up and returned to the pack for one more round.

2. **When I feel sad, talking to a friend cheers me up. --True**

When Evelyn worked at the Public Defender's office, we walked nightly to the jail to see whatever clients we couldn't counsel in the tank at court. Afterwards, we slumped into Jonny-O's to drink off the day and lard ourselves with Happy Hour food. We commiserated and, when one of us was in trial, tried out our opening statements. When Jonny broke down the buffet, it was time to finish our vodkas and head home. It felt good to have someone to talk to, someone who made me less scared. The pace and stakes of felonies had staggered me and I no longer drank to take the edge off. I drank to get numb.

A month after my promotion, Evelyn informed me in a guilty voice that she had accepted a job with a corporate litigation firm. She was drowning in student loans, sick of squeaking by on the shit salary they paid us at the PD's office. We'd still see each other all the time, she promised.

"It's cool," I said. I bought her drinks to show what a good friend I was, that I wasn't worried at all about how I would survive in the cesspool without her.

3. **Love has disappointed me.   --True**

The first time we slept together, Frank bit my nipples until they bled, his thin white lips persisting despite my polite attempts to wriggle out of range. When he rammed inside me, I felt no pleasure except the relief in not being alone. He said things during sex like, "Nowhere to run, huh baby?" and "Filthy whore." It startled me at first, then I noticed I liked it. After a sissified groan, Frank pulled out of me, rolled over and launched into a peroration on himself. I had an awful feeling he might expect me to talk about myself, but he just wanted someone to hear his words. I realized I didn't want to listen. I had my own problems.

Frank had alcohol issues. Not an addiction like I had developed, but a problem. Whenever he drank he became a real asshole. On St. Patrick's Day, after too many green beers, we cut down an alley behind Jonny-O's, staggering back to my rented one-bedroom craftsman. Frank was ranting about the lawyers in his courtroom who had walked all over him and shown him no respect. I said he shouldn't take it personally, they were just standing up for their clients. That's when the back of his hand flew backwards and cracked me across the bridge of my nose, knocking me on my ass. I stayed put for a minute, trying to figure out what just happened. Frank kept walking.

The next morning the phone rang as I stared into the mirror, admiring my shiner and fingering the fragile azure skin around my eye.

"Hey," Frank said when I picked up. His voice sounded mopey and contrite, a puppy who pissed on the rug. "Sorry about what happened."

I didn't know what I was supposed to say.

"I was fucked up and . . . " Frank paused, waiting for me to speak.

I sat there, soaking up the silence.

"Listen, Janet. You're not going to tell anyone, are you?"

Frank was a Superior Court judge who heard criminal cases. He had served as a panelist on "The Ravages of Crystal Methamphetamine on the Criminal Justice System" at the Spring Symposium of the Los Angeles Trial Lawyers Association. Afterwards, Frank lingered over his martini, we got to talking, and he ended up coming home with me. Frank had a reputation for meting out stern lectures and maximum jail time to any domestic violence offender sentenced in his court.

I didn't speak, didn't hang up, and didn't stop seeing him.

The next time it happened, we were camping deep in the Santa Ynez mountains. Frank hadn't been drinking, he was just in a really bad mood. He shattered my right cheekbone and left me on the side of Highway 33 with my thumb in the air.

After that it became easy to avoid him. The presiding judge had quit assigning my cases to Frank when it became public knowledge we were sleeping together. I stopped going out, so I only had to worry about chance meetings in the echoing corridors of the Hall of Justice.

There weren't any.

4. *I have problems with authority.* --*True*

"Counsel, approach the bench."

I stepped across the courtroom with Luke Banderman, wondering what this was about. Judge Nelson was a grouchy bastard and former D.A. who made no effort to conceal his loathing of defense attorneys and the scum we represented. Nelson had lost use of his right leg after being shot in a hunting accident and for the past ten years presided from the bench in a wheelchair. Lawyers in my office called him "Ironside" behind his back.

Luke wore charcoal Prada, accented with a striped silk tie. *CourtTV* had picked up Luke's last murder trial and female viewers phoned in record numbers to inquire about his marital status. Luke spent every penny on his wardrobe, always prepared to reward his local fan base if *Eyewitness 5* stopped by for his opinion on that week's high profile homicide. Jurors and judges ate him up, but his Eddie Haskell demeanor stabbed beneath my skin.

"How much longer with this witness?" whispered Ironside when we reached the bench.

"Ten minutes," I said.

"Good. I have an appointment I need to get to. I understand this will finish the prosecution's case and the defense can call its first witness after lunch."

After I finished cross-examination, Ironside straightened up in his chair and flashed a row of brown teeth at the jury. "Ladies and Gentlemen, now seems like a propitious time for our lunch recess. You are excused until 1:30."

I motioned for my client, Carl Williams, to stand while the judge rolled down from the bench. Carl leaned in and whispered, "Does that mean we get to eat now? Or we don't get to eat?"

"Sshhh." I smiled at the jury as they filed out.

The bad news was that my client had hit a guy with his car in broad daylight while speeding and the guy had died. The good news was that Carl had only been going 42 in a 35 zone and had not been drunk or high. The D.A.'s office didn't care and charged my client with vehicular manslaughter, despite his clean record, steady janitorial job and wife and infant son. Luke Banderman wanted Carl in prison.

The really good news was that my investigation had revealed that the dead guy had been jaywalking, after stepping out of a bar at 2:00 p.m. on a Tuesday, a bar he frequented daily. The bartender, Les Weidl, recalled the alleged victim had consumed his usual afternoon trifecta of a beer and two bourbons. The really, really good news —as good as it got in my line of work— was that the dead guy had had eye surgery the day before the accident, a surgery that, according to his own doctor, could have impacted his vision and orientation when stepping out of a dark bar into the blinding afternoon sunshine. With this evidence, no jury in the world would convict Carl.

I was going to mop the floor with Luke Banderman.

5. *Sometimes I feel nothing ever goes right for me.* --*True*

I scrambled to my office. I had sixty minutes to meet with my doctor and bartender witnesses, neither of whom were thrilled to testify, finalize my direct examination, scarf down some food, race back to meet Carl and answer his inevitable questions and be ready to go at 1:30 on the dot or risk getting chewed out by Ironside in front of the jury.

I stared in disbelief at the empty conference room.

"Where's Mr. Weidl and Dr. Spradley?" I asked the receptionist.

"Who?"

"Weidl! Spradley! My witnesses! Where are they?"

"Janet, nobody's checked in for you."

I tried to calm myself, hoping they had gone directly to court. I rifled through my file to see where I had ordered them to appear. A jolt of panic hit as I found the subpoenas, in triplicate, in the back of the file. My secretary had prepared the subpoenas, but I had stuffed them in the file and forgotten to have them served. Without proper service, neither witness had any obligation to testify, and neither would do it voluntarily. Each had made that abundantly clear. Without their testimony, Carl was doomed.

"Fuck!" I screamed and ran to find help, but the office was deserted. I called the bar, but Weidl had gone fishing. I called the surgeon, but he was in surgery. Two star witnesses unreachable because I had failed to subpoena them. This was a fuck up of epic proportions.

6. *Sometimes I want to smash things.* --*True*

"Your Honor, the defense seeks a recess until tomorrow afternoon." In a chambers conference, I confessed to Luke and Ironside what had happened, detailing the exculpatory testimony these witnesses would give. I told them about the subpoenas. I told them it was all my fault.

"Your Honor, we object to a continuance of any length," Luke said.

Ironside shook his head. "There will be no continuance, counsel."

"But Your Honor, without this testimony my innocent client is certain to be convicted. My failure to subpoena these witnesses will constitute grounds for a reversal of the conviction due to ineffective assistance of counsel—"

"Not my problem, counsel. Call a witness or we move to closing statements."

I argued. I fought. I made a complete record of my incompetence. Back inside the courtroom, Carl slouched in his borrowed suit. Ironside had allowed me five minutes to explain to my client how he would now go to prison because of my fuck up. Carl would likely only serve half the sentence before it got reversed on appeal. As Carl absorbed the news, I glanced around the courtroom at the bailiff, Ironside's clerk, Luke. The Hall of Justice henchmen loved gossip and news of my monumental screw up would spread like wildfire. I tried to enjoy the final moments of having been a semi-respected trial lawyer.

With no witnesses to call, we launched into closing arguments. The jury came back with a guilty verdict forty minutes later. At the office, I confessed to Henry, who grimaced and dialed the County's malpractice insurance carrier.

I was having a bad year. In addition to committing malpractice and torpedoing my career, my father had started spitting up blood again, something that's not technically supposed to happen to someone in remission. He went to the doctor and confirmed what I already knew. The cancer had returned. This time, with a vengeance.

7. *I try to act polite, even when others are critical.* --*True*

Driving home from work, my head throbbed. I was out of vodka and had no choice but to stop and refuel.

The Safeway parking lot swarmed with cars and as I turned down a packed aisle, I realized I was heading the wrong direction. "Shit," I whispered under my breath.

Another car started up the row, driving the proper direction, and a twinge of guilt prickled my skin. The asshole in this scenario was me and I hated being the asshole. I had been the asshole all day, as Carl Williams would certainly agree.

I spied an open parking place. As I steered hard to maneuver into the awkward angle, the car from the end of the aisle gunned it, braking with a screech an inch from my bumper.

"That was my spot, you fucking bitch!" the driver screamed.

Even in the falling darkness, I could see blackheads riddling her flattened nose. Gray streaked hair hung from under a Minnie Pearl hat and I couldn't help looking for a dangling price tag. "Sorry." I heard my voice sound sheepish. I'd felt sorry all day. No, all year. When would I stop feeling sorry for everything?

A car behind Minnie Pearl honked and she responded with a stiff and defiant middle finger.

"You fucking cunt!" she shrieked at me again. Her venom pierced my skin and soaked through to my spinal cord. She lurched into another space, climbed out of her car, and hovered near it. She was still yelling, but I couldn't make out the words. Finally she ambled toward the market entrance and the glass doors and bright lights swallowed her up. As I started to step out of my car, I realized I hadn't turned off the engine or unfastened my seatbelt. I sat for a minute and watched my hands tremble on the wheel.

At home I drank my Stoli, playing the confrontation over in my head, weighing the Dali Lama retort against the Sonny Corleone. But really, it wasn't my fault, I wanted to say. It was an innocent mistake. I'm a good person. People used to like me.

I took a Vicodin, left over from Frank, and started to feel better.

8. *I have a healthy appetite.*   *--False*

I stared at my reflection in the refrigerator door. We had a four-day Fourth of July weekend and I had spent mine on the couch, watching *Gilligan's Island*. I hadn't showered in three days and a stain bled across my sweatshirt where yesterday's coffee had managed to miss my mouth.

After ruining Carl's life and my reputation, and what with everything else, it had gotten hard to get out of bed. I started biting my nails, stopped showing up at parties, drank at home instead of Jonny-O's. Evelyn left messages I didn't return and eventually she stopped calling.

I opened the refrigerator and peered inside. The slick white sides were still spotless after the scouring they received during a brief misguided bout with sobriety. The shelves held a shriveled plum and four cans of Coors.

Someone told me that my father dropped a beer can on my head when I was three. He was rummaging the fridge for the minced ham, unaware I had pattered after him into the kitchen. I had no recollection of this and didn't know if it was true, though my father was a clumsy man and I did have an odd dent in my skull. I closed the door and poured all four Coors down my throat, wondering. Did I drink because my life was fucked up? Or was my life fucked up because I drank?

9. *Evil spirits possess me.*   *--True*

I had just turned ten in 1974 when Hollywood unleashed *The Exorcist*. Despite my parents' sheltering, I had still learned the movie contained images so disturbing that theatres provided "Exorcist Barf Bags," patrons fainted during screenings, and a San Francisco woman committed suicide after watching it. Theatres across the country hired security guards to ward off the twin evils of hysteria and six figure liability.

Four weeks earlier, my mother had packed up and left, leaving not so much as a note and my father was desperate to maintain some semblance of normalcy in my life. This meant a lot of things to my father but on a windy March Saturday, it meant spending his day off standing watch outside Food Basket where I peddled candy with six other Camp Fire Girls.

Food Basket stood next to the Pacific Theatre where *The Exorcist* was playing. Between customers, I watched my father slit his eyes in the direction of movie-goers offering tickets to a velour-clad usher. He paced between me and the other Camp Fire Girls, hands stuffed in his pockets, relaxing only when the last of the patrons disappeared into air-conditioned darkness. When my father trotted to the car for another case of Almond Rocca, I stole an opportunity to study the poster beneath the marquee. The scene of a man holding a briefcase under the shadows of a lamp post revealed nothing. But the message fueled my fears: "Nobody expected it, nobody believed it and nobody could stop it. The one hope, the only hope: THE EXORCIST."

After we closed up shop for the day, my friend Tess Thompson and I accompanied my father inside Food Basket. While Dad shopped, we made a beeline for the magazines to peruse *Teen Beat* and *Tiger Beat*, periodicals our parents refused to buy for us. Tess flipped the soft grainy pages past photos of Donny Osmond to the Cinema section. On the page was a benign photo of a girl in a white nightgown, propped against pillows in her bed, looking expectantly at a priest. "Linda Blair in *The Exorcist*," read the caption. Another jolt of fear hit my chest. Tess read aloud, "When the priest enters, the room is bitter cold—a sure sign of evil."

"I don't get it," I said, my voice wavering.

Tess was a tubby, pug-nosed girl. She smelled faintly of rotting cheese, but her self-esteem dwarfed mine. "She's possessed, dummy."

"Possessed?"

"By Satan." Tess hissed the *ssss* and widened her eyes for effect. "And it's a true story, you know."

Tess explained with her usual authority that Satan frequently entered the bodies of girls our age, he generally avoided Catholics (Tess happened to be Catholic), and gravitated toward sinners. She pointed to a *Tiger Beat* caption listing additional signs of possession —unusual strength and levitation.

Then Tess dropped the bomb. "The girl it happened to? You know, that the movie's about? She came from a broken family." Tess paused and leveled her eyes on me. "Just like you."

"Girls, let's go," my father called as he steered a grocery cart past us. Tess shoved *Tiger Beat* back into the rack and we ran to the parking lot.

That night, as I got ready for bed, my room felt cold.

"It's chilly in here, isn't it?" I asked when my father came to kiss me goodnight.

"Then get under the covers."

"In fact, it's bitter cold, wouldn't you say?"

"Don't be ridiculous," he huffed, "Good night." He snapped off the light and went to bed.

"Dad?" I stage whispered.

"Go to sleep!" he yelled. My father was a patient man, but not when it came time for sleep.

I lay in the dark, heart pounding, desperate to gauge the temperature, trying to convince myself I wasn't *that* strong. My mind raced with visions of priests waving crosses over me, chanting in Latin, then stepping out to our kitchen to shake their heads silently at my father. I saw my face transformed into a demon, head spinning on my neck, mouth spewing bile. Doom settled over me as I realized that not only were we not Catholic, we weren't religious at all. I had attended Missionary Christ Temple after two men holding gold-trimmed bibles knocked on our door one Saturday. The clean cut gentlemen offered free rides in their van to and from Sunday School and my mother jumped at the offer. I attended for two months until one Sunday, my eyes closed in prayer, someone stole my collection plate money from my purse. I never returned. One little set back and I had turned my back on God. Clearly, I was a sinner.

My world had turned upside down when my mother left, but now, as I lay awake in my bed, everything made sense in my ten-year-old mind. I was possessed by Satan and my mother had seen it. What would my father do when he learned why his wife had left? He could never forgive me and he would inevitably leave me too.

For months, the terror of my secret controlled me. I withdrew, spending hours at the mirror, searching for the signs of Satan my mother had seen, often finding evil in my shining eyes. Violating his principles, my father sent me to a child psychiatrist, a fat man with Dumbo-like ears who insisted that I act out dramas of abandonment with dolls. I gave him what he wanted, even confessed to a fear of the dark, but I guarded my secret. My mother had already left. I planned to hold on to my father for as long as I could.

10. I would enjoy working as a librarian.   --False

Carver Junior High School maintained the typical 1970s Southern California teen social hierarchy. Those groups divided first by race: Blacks, Whites, Mexicans, Vietnamese. White kids then roughly sub-categorized into Dorks, Brains, Jocks, Surfers, and Stoners. I was nervous and over-eager, features that ensured my Dork status. My eighth grade year had begun miserably when I started my period without realizing it. I walked all over campus with a stain seeping across the seat of my white Dittos until Ms. McElroy, the gym teacher, pulled me into the bathroom and explained what had happened.

Halfway through the school year, a campus cop caught Danny Green and I smoking pot behind the handball courts. On my behalf, my shamed father negotiated a punishment of three days suspension and a semester with Mr. Lazarro, Senior Librarian. Mr. Lazarro oversaw detention, an extra period tacked onto six regular class hours of the school day, for extra cash, he told us kids. Mr. Lazarro had a face like an owl and wore skin-tight polyester bell bottoms and platform shoes. Under his watch every afternoon, the girls sat on one side of the room where we flipped our feathered hair and fingered puka shell necklaces, writing each other notes and swinging freshly shaved legs. Guys sat on the other side, drawing lightning bolts or staring off into space. My crime had proven a turning point, giving me entrée into the elite society of Stoners, a networking opportunity that would shape my teenage years.

My mother resurfaced that year, phoning after four years of silence, brimming with tearful apologies, asking if she could still be part of my life. I rode the Number 7 bus to her apartment the day after her call. Her one room home was a dim hole. It bordered an alley emitting sounds of homeless men dumpster diving and pulverizing each other with angry fists. I pretended it didn't depress me while my mother fed me jelly donuts and two percent milk. She sat across from me, chain smoking Virginia Slims, her mouth twitching smiles and peppering me with questions. Did I like school? Did I have a boyfriend? For three months I visited her every Monday, her one day off from The Chicken Pie Shop, where she waitressed for minimum wage and fifteen percent of $2.99 Early Bird specials. Then she lost weight. She quit talking when I came over. She finally told me to stop coming at all.

I broached the subject with my father that night at dinner. "Dad, can Mom come live with us? I think she needs us now."

"What's done can't be undone," my father said and sat down to eat. His quivering lip belied his stern tone.

Serving out my sentence in detention, I wondered. Did Mr. Lazarro aspire to become a junior high librarian? Or was it just the space he landed after a downward spiral, complete with compromises and justifications? Between breaking up occasional fights and stepping outside to sneak a smoke, Mr. Lazarro sat at his desk reading *Popular Mechanics* while we delinquents copied text from *The Encyclopedia Britannica*, intending to pass it off in Social Studies as carefully researched reports. Afterwards, I studied *Seventeen Magazine*, straining to uncover the secrets of teen popularity. At the end of the year, we wrote sentimental words with undercurrents of truth in each other's yearbooks:

Janet, I didn't talk to you to much this year, but your a really sweet person. Elyse
Janet, Glad we became friends. Sure hope we stay that way. Joey
Janet, Watch out for the guys —they're sly devils! Love ya, Nance

On the last day of school, I felt a twinge of nostalgia saying goodbye to Mr. Lazarro, then shrugged it off as I came home to get ready for the Eighth Grade dance. I inserted my key in the lock, but the door swung open before I could turn it and I practically fell inside the house. I looked up to see my father's ashen face. He was home early from work, something that had never happened before.

"What's wrong?" I asked.

He sat down at the kitchen table and put his face in his thick hands, muffling sobs. "Your mother killed herself," he said, his voice cracking. He had never stopped wearing his gold wedding band and in that moment it seemed to burn on his finger.

That was the day I learned to expect the worst.

11. After a rough day, I need a few drinks to relax.   --True
"Celebrating the last weekend of summer with a party?" asked the check out girl.

"Yeah," I lied.

I now purchased my vodka in the economical 1.75 liter size with the handle fused into the glass. Booze was the only thing I could count on, my reward for making it through another work day of assholes whispering behind my back. Booze washed away everything, even my father's decay, a decay which had demanded hospitalization.

But as of late, it had stopped working and that terrified me. Each night I sat on my couch, twisting the edges of the afghan my mother had knitted twenty years earlier. I tugged the fringe, like my anxiety, tighter and tighter, winding the strands so they wouldn't come apart. I drank more, washing down the Vicodin my body now screamed for. But even then I couldn't get any relief.

12. Sometimes things happen that terrify me.   --True
Halloween night, the ICU nurse called and said to come quick, it looked like it was time for him to go. I sped over streets slick with rain to the hospital

and jogged through empty fluorescent halls to ICU. Outside my father's room, I put on the thin rubber gloves and yellow paper gown I had been ordered to wear.

My father was unconscious and his left hand twitched, scratching the white sheet, dark tubes trailing behind like eels swimming in blue shadows of the room. He had suffered in this room for a month, intubated with a coiling tube strapped to his face, its flesh-colored plastic like the kind in Hannibal Lecter's mask. I tried to count the needles and tubes crammed into his nose, throat, arms, urethra, and gave up. I placed my hand over his, but sequestered behind a sheath of rubber, I was separated from my father's touch.

When I had visited earlier, the tube down his throat prevented speech, but his blue eyes sparked and he grasped my hand tighter than ever before. The other hand, tubes dangling, gestured in a made up sign language I couldn't understand. He raised his arm chest level and arched his hand in a fluttering movement like a bird. I blurted out guesses, not bothering to consider whether they made any sense.

"How was my flight?"

He shook his head no.

"You had pigeon for dinner?"

His face crumpled in grim amusement, then he resorted to writing letters in the air with his finger tip, spelling out words, but I couldn't follow those either. He let his hand drop to the bed with a flop. I feared my first guess was close, that he signed about one of us going away, but I couldn't venture that aloud. I didn't have a tube in my mouth, but I couldn't speak either. Instead I held his hand and we stared into each other's eyes, making up for the words we never said.

But he didn't die. Actually, he got better. They removed the breathing tube, and then the feeding tube. He moved to a regular hospital room, then hospice.

"Your father survived the infection, but he's still dying," said his rumpled doctor.

"I know," I heard myself sounding defensive.

"Hospice will do everything they can to keep him comfortable, but I'm not going to lie to you. Your father will experience significant pain."

I nodded, thinking back two years earlier, before the cancer appeared and began its campaign of destruction. He had slipped in the garage and broken his hip. Nurses confided to me in hushed tones with traces of accusation that my father had an extremely low pain threshold. What did that mean, anyway, I had demanded. Sure they could measure outward manifestations of experience from a career full of patients, but how could they feel what another person felt? How did they know? Maybe it really feels more painful for him, I had said. They shook their heads and shot each other knowing glances. I didn't understand, their eyes said. I didn't know the things they knew.

13. My judgment feels better than ever.   --False

A month later, at hospice, I sat with my dad. As of that morning, he had a private room because his roommate had died (loudly, according to my father) at 3:06 a.m. in the bed five feet away. The man's body sat there until two morning shift orderlies wheeled it past my father as he sat propped up in bed, trying to swallow lukewarm tea and runny eggs. We sat, not speaking, until my father broke the silence.

"I want to ask you something." His voice rasped, his throat still raw from intubation.

"What, Dad?"

"A favor."

"Okay." I waited to hear what he could possibly need.

"I'm dying."

"Yeah, I know."

The room swelled with silence.

"I want you to help me."

"Sure, Dad. Anything. Just tell me what you need."

"I want you to . . . " his throat chafed, making me wince. "I want you to help me die."

"What?"

His eyes closed and I watched his throat move as he swallowed.

"Kill me. I want you to kill me, honey." He paused. "Please."

"Jesus, Dad."

"There's a way to do it. You won't get in trouble."

"That's not exactly my biggest concern."

He didn't answer. I sat still, trying to think of what to say.

"Can I think about it Dad?"

He closed his eyes and lay incredibly still, his chest barely rising with his breath. Then he opened his eyes and stared like he couldn't quite place me.

"Sure." He closed his eyes again. "But don't take too long."

I sat in stunned quiet, staring at the floor. When I looked up, he was asleep.

The request gnawed my stomach as I drove home. I wanted to do right here, but what was right? Follow the rules and let my father suffer a pain I couldn't imagine? Or kill him? Could I live with myself if I did this? Could I live with myself if I didn't? At home I poured a drink. It was asking a hell of a lot. But that was why I had to do it. How didn't matter. I would figure that part out later.

I had made my decision but still couldn't sleep. I tossed and turned and doubt swelled inside my throat. Who was I kidding? Right or wrong, there was no way I could go through with this.

14. I know that I am loved and there will always be someone who cares for me.   --False

The next morning, hospice called. They were sorry to inform me that my father had passed away. He died peacefully, they lied.

I made arrangements. My father wanted to be cremated, no funeral, no wake, saving the humiliation of a low turnout. A single parent and taciturn to the point of rudeness, my father had few friends. Those he'd had died before him or were themselves too sick to leave their beds. He was a widower and an only child, so that just left me.

"Looks like you're down to just one person in this world," Frank had said when he rode out of my life for good.

"Fuck you," I shot back. It was a shitty thing to say, calculated to hit hard and reverberate to the tips of my nerve endings. But he was right.

And now I was down to none. Now I was an orphan. Thirty years old maybe, but an orphan nonetheless. And it was in that selfish moment of untethered fear, panic in having no one at all, that everything unraveled.

15. When things go wrong, I feel like giving up.   --True

I couldn't sleep. I could not stop thinking about my father. It pained me to not know where he was, whether he was all right. Dr. Nguyen prescribed Ambien, Xanax, Valium. I swallowed the pills, grateful for Dr. Nguyen's generosity, and lay down with my frayed afghan to pray for rest.

16. My father was a good man.   --True

I saw my father standing in the driveway as I pulled in, home early from work. He stood there in a crisp white shirt, pressed khakis, tasseled brown loafers. Tan and spry, his eyes twinkled like he was up to something. Then I blinked and he disappeared.

I woke that night from coerced sleep and stepped through shadows to the bathroom. A breeze lifted the tiny hairs on the back of my neck and I asked the darkness, "Dad?" But he didn't answer.

"Dad, if you're there, say something." I stood frozen in the hall, waiting. "Dad, I want to talk to you. I promise I won't be scared."

I walked back from the bathroom, still searching for signs of him, but there was nothing. When I crawled back into bed I spoke the truth to the darkness, inviting him to appear in my driveway looking happy and fit.

"Those are words I haven't used to describe you in years, Dad. What made you such a model of stability? You stood at the stove frying hamburger patties, browning tater tots. Every night you had us at the dinner table at six sharp. You asked about my day. Did I need help with homework? Money for school supplies? If you drank, it was only in moderation. How could you stop at just one glass of burgundy? A single can of Budweiser? You were a good man. How can I possibly be your daughter?"

A knife-like sob stopped my eulogy. I rocked back and forth, crying in my private little vortex of tragedy.

"Daddy don't leave me," I whispered over and over, until I finally fell into the soft forgiving fog of sleep.

17. I'm as motivated to work as I ever was.   --False

A noise rippled, then rolled waves through my head. The sound rose, gathered shape, and I recognized the ring of a phone. I mumbled into the receiver.

"Janet? Is that you?" said a voice.

I moved my lips and tongue to form words but choked and slipped into coughs.

"Janet?"

I dropped the phone and coughed until I caught my breath. I recognized my bed, and sunlight peeking through blinds.

"Janet, are you there? It's Diane . . . from the office? . . . Goddamnit, will you say something please? The court called. Again. You missed all of your morning appearances. The presiding judge talked to Henry." There was a long pause. "Henry's pissed, Janet."

I eased myself into a sitting position. My crotch felt damp and I thought I had peed myself, but the wetness inside my flannels was thick, sticky and I realized it was blood. The stain seeped from my crotch into the sheet, enormous and pure crimson. It reminded me of a crime scene.

"Did you hear what I said?"

"Tell him I'm sick." My throat felt like I had been drinking sand.

"We've been telling him that for two months. No one in this office wants to cover your appearances anymore and you knew damn well you were supposed to show up today."

I had nothing to say.

"The presiding judge is reporting you to the state bar and Henry said he's got no choice but to fire you."

The voice stopped talking and I hung up and went back to sleep. Day became night, then day again. Or maybe it was one endless day. I woke up to peek inside the refrigerator, have a drink, take a pill, then went back to sleep. First I lost days. Then weeks.

18. I have uncontrollable fits of laughter and tears.   --True

By December, Dr. Nguyen said he couldn't help me anymore and passed me off to a colleague, Dr. Blume.

Warm stereo speakers piped "Soft Rock from the '70s" into the antiseptic reception area where I listened to Jackson Browne, Elton John and ABBA, hoping like hell this Blume could relieve the throbbing assault at the back of my skull. I listened to those songs the year my mother disappeared, the year I tumbled down an icy black abyss. Tapping my foot, I decided oldies comfort us because we can hear a song from twenty years ago, unfiltered by the nerve-searing shit we were going through at the time. The haze of nostalgia gave the gift of knowing that one particular period of hell was finally over.

I pondered this as John Denver sang *Annie's Song*. My father bought me that album in an unprecedented retail therapy spree after my mother took off. I played it to make him happy, but I'd hated it. It depressed me that millions of people heard those clichéd lyrics as some shiny expression of love. This insight had made me feel even more alone. I must have been an odd kid.

I started crying then, but the fact that I was in a waiting room bawling over *Annie's Song* seemed funny somehow. A giggle escaped, then shifted into howls of laughter. I couldn't stop. I doubled over. It scared the shit out of me.

My laughter melted back into gasping sobs. I slid out of my chair onto the smooth industrial carpeting, the hard floor hurting my tailbone. As I wondered what the hell was wrong with me, a section of beige wall opened and a nurse appeared.

"The doctor will see you now."

19. I often dream about things best kept to myself.   --True

I'm sitting alone with my father on a metal bench in a deserted stadium covered in snow. A hidden sun emits gray light, turning the snow to ash. We wear hats, gloves and parkas but still shiver. A snowflake falls on my face and warms my cheek. My father sits motionless, but not waiting, the way he waited his whole life. His body doesn't lurch with currents of pain and in this moment I don't worry.

But a shifting burdens my peace. Necessity. A need for words. I summon courage to speak, to say what I need to say. I'm holding a rectangular eyeglass case and the lines etched on it match the corrugated lines on the bench where I sit by my father, our knees touching. My father points to the case. He looks into my eyes and reaches for it, then grips it with surprising strength.

"Don't." I tug it back, but he won't let go. He holds on, pulling with unfamiliar insistency as tendons clench in my neck. I'm not sad about what I have to tell him. I only want to inflict the least amount of pain.

"Dad . . . " I stop.

Tell me, his eyes say. Tell me what you need to say.

"Dad, I did it." I gesture with the case. "I'm dead. These are my ashes." As if on cue, a fleck of my former self escapes through the seam. It swirls upward with the snow and then disappears.

My father's face contorts like it did the day my mother died and his mouth croaks out words. "No. Undo it. Undo it right now." He shoves me off the bench and I start to fall.

I wake as my body hits my bedroom floor. I'm gasping for air and crawl up to snap on the lamp to erase the dream. The mess of empty amber bottles on the nightstand reminds me what's real. What the fuck have I done?

I dial the phone and hear a voice. "911 operator, what's your emergency?"

When the ambulance comes, a paramedic shines a light in my eyes, asks me my name, what did I take?

He is young. Handsome, with eyes flecked in gold. He touches my arm and I grip his hand, holding it there, not willing to feel him let go. "You're okay," he says, "You're going to make it through."

And in that moment, all I want is to believe him.

———

MYSTERY DATE

Twitching with want, but doubting all I desired, I entered my phase of dangerous analogies, comparing people to pigs and national disasters. I got away with this because I myself resembled nothing. When I met someone new I sized them up, stabbing with educated guesses at what they regretted in their lives. It was still only 1976 and I was just twelve, but I knew already that the worst part of living was yearning for the things one's own choices had placed just out of reach.

Not surprisingly, most people learned to steer clear of me, especially the kids rungs beyond me in a junior high school social structure more intricate and dangerous than the jungle gyms I had climbed inside as a little girl. So alone in the dullness of my room, draped across the width of my bed, I lost myself inside books borrowed weekly from the Oak Park Public Library. Adrift inside their scenes I answered back to the characters in those pages, feeling all the things they felt. Tangled in the dark promise of a book, the sounds outside my window faded. I reveled in my ability to disappear for hours, to finally blink up from the page, disoriented, wondering, Where am I? Whose butterfly bedspread is this? Whose arms are these? Then I'd get a chill, followed by a lonesome pang like when someone you actually like forgets your name.

Catching me in conversation with myself more than once, my parents determined that I needed to get out of the house more, to work harder at forming sustainable relationships. *Forming sustainable relationships.* My father was a plumber, my mother a part-time waitress. They didn't use such words and I suspected they had consulted a shrink, or worse. People have a bad habit of looking back at adolescence with nostalgia, yearning for the freedom of simpler times. But a child has no freedom. You're commanded to leave your cage, then ordered to crawl back inside. You have only the illusion of choices, the option to select from whatever has been placed in front of you. In any event, it was through my parents' misdirected concern for my social development that I came to meet Mary Gerson and her family.

Catholic and severe, Mary's house felt almost as dull as mine. Mary's frog-faced father was a middle-aged insomniac. He organized the family garbage late at night, bagging shriveled remains of orange peels and dinner scraps so they didn't stain the copies of *Seventeen* discarded by his three daughters, each named after a saint. Mr. Gerson worked for the phone company but held a position that never required him to climb the poles that covered our neighborhood. He hid copies of *Playboy* in stacks of old newspapers in the garage and when confronted with them by Mary, explained he had purchased them for the articles.

Mr. and Mrs. Gerson seldom argued. Their worst fight occurred when Mrs. Gerson wanted to go out for ice cream and Mr. Gerson said he wasn't in the mood. Mrs. Gerson's face pinched to a pout and she sat in the living room with arms crossed tightly against her chest, watching TV in stony silence. After an hour, she made a production of slamming a bowl onto the kitchen counter and filling it with brown sugar. She sat on the floor at her husband's feet and ate the entire contents of that bowl, pretending to satiate her sudden need. It never occurred to Mrs. Gerson to pile her girls into her blue Pontiac and go out for ice cream herself.

I know all of this from becoming Mary's friend, from spending as much time inside the Gerson house as my own. The lure of Mary and her home were her older sisters, Veronica and Therese, who became my doorway to a different world and the source of my metamorphosis. These girls fought back. They refused to be caged and as a consequence had lived better and more interesting lives than Mary and I had so far. Veronica and Therese were our sole source of reliable information and we huddled on the floor of their room for as long as they let us. We begged for stories from their lives, mentally filing away facts we might take and use to create a better existence, an existence, it turned out, which required boys to have any meaning. Under their tutelage Mary and I learned to flip our feathered hair and finger puka shell necklaces, eyeing boys only from the corner of an eye, while casually swinging freshly shaved legs. The trick, Therese whispered, was to pretend that you just didn't care.

By the time summer came, our nipples pierced our halter tops with their own trapped aggression, and Mary and I learned together how to use those mysterious feminine products, packaged in pink and covered in promises. Lying on beach towels in our parents' driveways, we became desperate for a tan, to look like we had gone somewhere, done something with our summer. Saturdays we stayed inside while our fathers mowed the grass. Back and forth in tidy rows, they had something to show for their day while we retreated inside playing Canasta, removing our retainers to eat peanut butter on Wonder bread, watching *I Love Lucy* reruns. We could waste our days because we were filthy rich with time. Days were impossibly long and we had so many in front of us we couldn't possibly concern ourselves with spending them wisely.

On my thirteenth birthday, Mary watched me make a wish and blow out candles on a white frosted cake. Then she stared in silence as I opened my two gifts, a digital clock radio and Milton Bradley board game. We retreated to my room and under the watchful eye of my new clock, ripped the cellophane from the game. It was called Mystery Date. Open the door to find your perfect match! The box promised good clean fun and a peek into our dating future, though I knew its purpose was to drill our subconscious minds with skills necessary to identify the qualities that constituted an appropriate man.

As it turned out, there were not that many qualities to dream of in a man. My chance mates included a bland, square-headed boy in a crisp white dinner jacket, waiting to whisk me away to prom. Next came bowling alley dork, wearing goofy black framed glasses and red plaid pants, holding a matching bowling bag. Finally there was the bum, smudged in dirt, hands stuffed inside eternally empty pockets, a man whose eyes promised that years later he would habitually yell up from the downstairs couch that he was hungry, *when was I making those goddamn pancakes?*

The game proved simple. Open the door to a good guy and win. Get a dud and lose. But to me, each of these cardboard men held their own promise, the promise to get me out of my parents' stifling house, off their lime green polyester carpet that scratched at my skin. Any of them could give me what I most longed for but couldn't identify: an identity beyond myself. Mary assured me that I wanted the one in the dinner jacket and presented a cogent argument as to why. But alone, after Mary had been called home for dinner, I stared down into his flat eyes, willing him to speak.

--What can you offer me besides that corsage?

--Security.

--I'm thirteen. I don't even know what that means.

--It's nice. Marry me and you'll see.

I screamed that at thirteen, I didn't need to be saved, and security was synonymous with boredom. But the game just claimed to be doing its job, teaching me: You are offered a small assortment of realities and it is from these that you must choose.

--But what if I don't want to choose?

--You must.

--Why?

--Because those are the rules.

My mother tapped on the door and asked who I was talking to.

--No one. You must be hearing something outside.

I shoved Mystery Date in the back of my closet and vowed to have nothing to do with it. Alone again, I studied my new clock radio. So reliably hesitant, its little plastic tabs quivered, fighting before finally giving in and flipping over, surrendering to the passage of another minute. Eventually that clock betrayed me and time began to move faster.

That next year in school, Mary and I learned we had rights. So we declared our right to choose, and the right to change our minds about what we had chosen. We declared our right to keep and bear clove cigarettes, that the freedom of speech included the freedom to use the f-word any fucking time we felt like it, until our mothers told us to shut our filthy mouths and vacuum. Mothers sifting through our trash in the name of cleaning violated our Fourth Amendment rights, we proclaimed. So call the ACLU, our mothers said, blowing smoke at the ceiling. It turned out we had no rights at all, not even the right to cast a vote. But it didn't matter. In truth all we wanted at that point was the right to slow dance with an exquisite stranger, a dangerous mystery man who whispered secrets in our ears.

The next year we turned fifteen and Mary and I had a ménage a trois with a man who claimed to be a stand-in double on *Starsky & Hutch*. We didn't know which one he was supposed to be. We didn't care. And we didn't know yet about the girl-on-girl part of such arrangements, didn't know that was part of the deal. If we had known, we would have done it, but we didn't know. Licking us like cotton candy, pink and sticky, Starsky –or Hutch– got worn out. Too much work for one man I supposed. I shrugged, got dressed, went back to the party we had left. I was determined to keep moving, experimenting, sampling from what life had to offer. Mary and I had our whole lives ahead of us so we drove drunk, fucked the wrong men, skipped the scraping of our cervixes in the gynecological exams that promised to save our lives.

But later that same year, everyone in Mary's family took unwarranted turns. Therese had some kind of breakdown: Satan was inside her. Mr. and Mrs. Gerson suddenly consummated the sin of divorce. Veronica escaped to a small liberal arts college three thousand miles away, never looking back. It all left Mary on the edge, staring into an abyss. I was still trying so hard to get somewhere, anywhere, and the people I had come to love were struggling just to get back to the point where they had started. But they couldn't, because whether they liked it or not, everything had stopped. Everything except time, which kept running on without them.

Years later, the call from Mary's father was like being caught naked by an intruder. I sat in the dark quiet of my parents' empty house two nights before returning for my second year of college. The ring of the phone violated the stillness of the air, and I reached for it, paying no attention to what was about to happen.

His voice came on the line, speaking my name, explaining who was calling, though at that point I already knew. A jolt of fear electrified my insides. Something horrible had happened to Mary. Why else did a father call his daughter's friends? I felt my panic was justified. I had, after all, just returned from the hospital, visiting another childhood friend whose face had transformed to a giant scab, unrecognizable from having flown face first through the windshield of her boyfriend's car. No seatbelt, the nurse had said to me as I stared at the girl in horror. The nurse's tone was a warning for caution, her cold eyes leveling me before turning on a white wedged heel and disappearing silently from the room.

But as Mr. Gerson got to the point of his call, I learned Mary was fine. His voice, deeper, more gravelly, didn't hesitate.

--I was wondering if you'd like to join me for a drink.

Stuck on the other side now, middle-aged myself, I remember my youth. Looking back at my parents' house, I see it now as a haven. I close my eyes and picture it, remaking it with blackout windows and no doors. Looking back at those years I see only endless possibility because we all remember ourselves better than we were, and that is our right. Only after growing up do we realize that the Mystery Date game was only trying to help us, teaching us that while the details that put flesh to cardboard vary, the categories stay the same. How could I have known that one of those cardboard choices would include the father of my friend? Offering himself up to me, pressing his lips so hard into mine they bruised, tasting my saliva and sharing his. A relationship described briefly for what it was: a fly unbuttoning in the bathroom of a bar, ankles wrapped around a thick pale waist, a prim vow of silence. *Repeat as necessary.*

After a year with Mr. Gerson, my Mystery Date game turned out to include a cast of hundreds, featuring fun (but volatile) Meth man, followed by Wall Street man clutching handfuls of money in beefy paws, followed by Green man with bike and single reusable sandwich bag. After that came Recession-Depression man who worked his whole life only to lose everything, who then spent entire days in bed. And last but not least, Cancer man, dream date grown gaunt and hollowed with concave cheeks, tufts of hair falling from his head when I stroked it.

You can block out a person's life by the people they have been with. I know people who have stayed with the same person for thirty years, but that just makes their story shorter. Through my real life Mystery Dates I learned the hard way what questions to ask. How many people have you known? What's the worst thing you've ever done? How do you want to die? Have you ever given a pity-fuck? Do you fight dirty? Ever waved a gun over your head? What's your approach to debt? Just how disappointed are you with how things have turned out?

Mary and I, bodies throbbing with want, couldn't possibly have known that those girls who were us would disappear forever. We couldn't know then how much we would lose in our lives, that we would make new plans, adjust our dreams to fit the passage of time and what it had left us. We couldn't possibly have known how short time is, how it never comes back.

———

THE ASYMMETRICAL SCIENCE OF

LOVE

In the asymmetrical science of love, I am telling you the truth.[1]

I want you to know that I love you.[2]
And I want you to know where I was.[3]

And for you to admit cell phones are not infallible.[4]

I'm sorry you feel dingy.[5]

You don't understand.[6]

AllIwannadoishavesomefun.[7]
It is you who lives in self-exile.[8]

---

[1] With the understanding that truth can be relative.
[2] With the caveat that love sometimes means hate.
[3] Though the earth is always spinning, spinning, spinning, so it may not be possible to confirm my exact whereabouts.
[4] See Verizon Wireless Service Agreement, page 6, paragraph 4.
[5] But how can that be my fault?
[6] It's like you batter me senseless, then drag me across the lawn.
[7] before I die, says the man next to me out of nowhere.
[8] That might sound better in Latin.

You and I have a richly textured history.[9]

You've got to get over it.[10]

The heart wants what the heart wants.[11]

There, there.[12]

Do you want to grab some breakfast?

———

---

[9] I miss the way you used to be.
[10] As in, you only caught me that once.
[11] As in, look out for that cliff.
[12] *Oy Vey.*

COLLISION

It's my turn to deliver the eulogy.

I slump on the couch, scribbling in a Mead notebook purchased for the occasion. I read drafts to my sister Jaime, who smirks and shakes her head at each one.

"Too boastful."

"Too Hallmark-ey."

"Too pestilent."

Jaime lies prone on the dusty floor of my living room doing Pilates, so each critique comes out a grunt. She's doing that "swimming" move, her bony pelvis stuck flat to the floor, arms and legs stretched out straight and flapping like crazy, like there's a fucking shark chasing her. Her black hair covers her face and frames her skull in a web and for a second I believe she really is underwater.

I strain for what to say, something that sounds right. I tear shreds from the notebook, crumpling each white page hard and loud and throwing wadded balls tight and low across the room. Ripping paper from the spiral frazzles my nerves further and I pause, wondering if the Army forbids or merely frowns upon a widow drinking whiskey before the funeral.

I walk to the kitchen sink and open my mouth beneath the tap. I tongue the water, forcing the stream in different directions.

"You're disgusting," Jaime says, "Use a glass."

Through the window above the sink I can see into my neighbor's kitchen. A new kid, shipping out next week. Corporal Somebody. He stands at his own sink, naked except for a towel around his waist, tearing off chunks of grocery store rotisserie chicken with his hands and shoving the meat inside his mouth. He's gnawing at the flesh of a leg when he sees me staring. He gives a nod of recognition with his greasy chin.

"Why do people die?" I murmur, still staring out the window.

Jaime drops her swimming legs to the floor with a thud. She sucks in her breath, then exhales, blowing hair off her face. "Duh. It's a key component in the cycle of life."

Corporal Somebody thinks I'm talking to him and knits his brows into a jagged wand, forming a single word around a mouthful of dark meat, "*What?*"

I shake my head and he mouths something else, something that looks like "*Sorry*," and this time I nod.

Jaime walks toward me wearing her softest face. "Come on. You're not the first person to lose someone in a war." This is Jaime's best attempt at comfort.

She pauses, shifts her voice to an upbeat gear. "Hey, I was at a service last week and the chaplain said, 'Death is the collision between this world and the next.'" Jaime holds my chin and tilts my face so I have to meet her gaze. "Maybe you should steal that?"

When we're dressed and ready to leave, my heart beats in measures, a steady tempo of doom. At the door I clutch Jaime's hand and beg her, *Tell me*. On today of all days, why must I be the one to spill the contents of my heart?

———

RESCUE

The river is my retreat when I've been lied to by men.

Camping at the edge, I ignore the dung colored water, focusing instead on the blooming bushes on the banks of the other side, bushes bursting with the weight of some dark ripe fruit I have never tasted, berries nestled between clusters of thorns and flinging themselves from the vine to litter the water's surface, black sticky globs oozing like blood.

Ambling alone through the trails at dusk I become aware that something will happen soon, the kind of something that might change me.

I don't have to wait long before I hear the gurgled screams, panicked words bubbling through water demanding *HELP*.

When I jump into the vast murkiness of the river, I believe I can save her. But as I swim within reach her hands clasp my head like I'm a buoy, pushing me deep into the black water. I know drowning people are dangerous because in their panic, their desperation to save their own life, they willingly take the life of their would-be rescuer. I fight, struggling back to the surface, gasping for air when her hands grab again at my head, fingers pressing into the bones of my skull, hoisting her heavy water-logged body onto my shoulders, forcing me to slide back under into the dark nothingness where I continue to sink. Water fills my mouth, forcing its way down my throat, choking me. I can't believe my arrogance, my certainty I could save a drowning woman. Her limbs clutch at me, and I struggle to get free, feeling her body absorb the force of my kicks. Head bobbing at the surface, she shouts words I can't understand. She swings at me, the base of her wrist connecting with the flatness of my temple. I climb her body like a rope while she squirms to push me off. I press her head underwater and hold it, feeling her fight start to go, watching the bubbles get smaller until finally, they stop.

For a long time I sit at the edge next to the dead girl, throwing stones into the water, enjoying the sound they make when they hit the surface before they disappear. Floating face up she looks almost peaceful, even with her face bloated, flies darting at her swollen eyes. I imagine the thick nauseating zip of the black bag that will make her disappear, EMTs in pressed white shirts, their boots sucking away through the red mud, knees buckling from the weight of the girl who taught me it's safe to be a rescuer, that I won't be brought down.

I stand and walk back through the darkness all the way into town. I'm ready to hear the sound of deep baritone voices. I need to hear them. I need them to lie to me some more.

———

CHRONOLOGY

You drift into my no-fly zone, demanding I corrupt you.
You explain the structure of the universe.
You use words like *incandescent*.
I confess my sins: trying too hard, wanting too much.
Everything becomes too bright and big.
I disappear into the cave of your heart.

You teach me how the best lies have layers of truth.
My whites turn to gray.
I use words like *forage*.
I want to leave.
"Come here," you say. You won't let me go.
Your face is a jigsaw puzzle, all dark sky, impos-
sible to piece together except the hard edges.
"Go away," you say.
You tear off my limbs, slowly, careful not to rip beyond their perforated
edges. "They were made for this," you say, severing while I watch.

Caller ID labels you *Unknown.*
I put a tracking device on your heart. The green
light blinks. *Tracing…Tracing,* it promises.
Lies less subtle.
I'm a car that's been keyed.
I turn the other cheek.
I turn, and I turn, until I'm shaking my head *No.*

———

THE RULE AGAINST PERPETUITIES

Flunking the bar exam had resurrected my failure as a first year law student when the Dean summoned me to his office to discuss "what went wrong" to trigger such a "disappointing performance" in my Real Property class.

"Tammy, what happened?" he had asked as I sat across from him, tugging at the ends of my frizzy black hair.

What happened is that I had fallen victim to the Rule Against Perpetuities, a legal principle made incomprehensible by its ticking clock and future contingencies. The Rule restricted gifts to future generations, demanding that ownership transfer within a strict period after the death of someone alive when the gift was bequeathed. "Alive" included persons conceived but not yet born, creating easily overlooked realities like unborn widows and fertile octogenarians. The Rule tolerated uncertainty for only so long and violations carried harsh consequences: the gift was voided and given to someone else. Put to the test, I couldn't untangle exam questions about the Rule. I searched multiple choice answers to select from *a* through *e*, but each choice had merit and my identification of the best answer had proven inadequate.

I told the Dean none of this and served out my sentence as a first year law student on academic probation. Violating the law school policy prohibiting first year students from working part time jobs had contributed to my academic demise, but fifteen hours a week at Ragi's Neighborhood Drycleaner earned me enough to close the gap left by federal student loans. I had hit the floor whenever classmates entered the chimed front door, I stole time from spotting stains and making change to read *Prosser on Torts*, and I struggled. Working explained a fraction of my failure, nothing more. I came from another world and had gone to law school to break free, but that first year was filled with painful recognition, a time of comprehending that I was different from my peers. They possessed something I lacked, something more than clothes, cars and cash.

Now my second chance, the 1990 California Bar Exam, loomed three weeks away and the Rule Against Perpetuities still tormented me. All I had figured out was that the Rule's intricacies existed because things with heirs never go as expected and assumptions rarely proved true, usually because we hadn't considered all the possibilities. But instead of hitting the law library, I now headed toward the Sunnyside Convalescent Center. I could hardly afford this visit, but threats of another failure withered beneath the shame that throbbed my forehead until I promised myself I would come today.

I stepped inside to Sunnyside's dim light and feculent odor, thick in motionless air. Not pausing to allow my eyes to adjust, I marched head down to the reception desk and an assortment of languid nurse's aides. The aides were white, black, Hispanic, Filipino, Vietnamese. They wore playful scrubs adorned with teddy bears or Hello Kitty and shared the same sour expression. One squatted on a stumpy swivel chair, her dimpled thighs torturing the fabric of white polyester pants as she avoided eye contact and pantomimed work. A clipboard held a long empty list where I printed *Tammy Warner*, then signed my name again in the next column as instructed. I checked the clock, entered the time, filled in Name of Patient Visited and left the Relationship column blank.

Circling from the desk, I trudged down a bile green corridor, its walls decorated only with gray light. A man hunched over a walker, inching forward like a determined insect past shrunken bodies slumped in wheelchairs lining the hall. Some flashed toothless smiles and reached out twisted claws, craving human touch. Some muttered like lunatics, while others searched in vain for the frazzled, impatient son who promised to visit but never showed.

Across the threshold of Room 4-J lay Aunt Gracie. She was awake, her bones encased by a sheath of moth-like skin and propped upright by a mechanical bed unadorned with the beeps or digital flickering of medical equipment. A miniature milk carton teetered on the edge of a flesh colored tray and a substance masquerading as meat sat in a gelled pool of grease next to string beans and an ashen paste. The meal's odor mingled with the scent from the hall and my forehead prickled with sweat.

She looked at me through milky brown eyes set against blue tinted skin. "Hi honey," her voice croaked.

"Hi," I bent to kiss a papery cheek, "Sorry it's been so long."

Hollows of collar bone peeked out of her stained hospital gown and bony shoulders formed sharp points at its edges. Splashes of magenta covered her arms, leaking stories of incompetent nurses jabbing needles in search of a blood yielding vein. Gracie's eight husbands and countless boyfriends, all dead or otherwise forgotten long before she turned sixty, the same year I was born, now seemed altogether mythical.

Gracie was make-upless, a condition that still startled me on these visits. I expected to see the face of my childhood: the thick layer of Maybelline shine-free foundation that formed a canvas for rouge dusted cheeks, rainbows of eye shadow, false eyelashes tangling with each blink and cherry lips that clamped a lit PallMall. With an economy sized can of AquaNet, she had lacquered her dyed black hair into a helmet until 1978 when she marched into the Citrus Grove Beauty Shop and demanded that the geriatric gay man behind the counter give her a Dorothy Hamill hair cut and a blow job.

"You mean blow dry, don't you, sweetie?" he had corrected.

"Whichever," she had told him, settling into his chair.

Now I searched her face, longing to find the woman who took me to my first concert at age seven. The woman who unleashed feverish screams when Engelbert Humperdinck crooned *Release Me* and who let go of my hand only long enough to hike down red satin panties from beneath a paisley minidress. She leaned on my shoulder in the crowd for support as she stretched them over the heels of patent leather boots and launched them at the stage of the Civic Theatre.

On the evenings my parents had attended bowling league award dinners, postal employee Christmas parties and other blue-collar spectacles, she baby-sat me in her Section 8 apartment, always redolent with *Charlie!* perfume. We scoffed at my bed time and huddled together on a scratchy plaid sofa under crocheted afghans where we feasted on buttered popcorn and Cokes and watched *Canon, Mannix, Emergency!, Mary Tyler Moore* and any beauty pageant ever televised. I would watch her, awash in the television glow, as she discharged a string of expletives at the unjust elimination of Miss New Mexico. I stared as she trembled and shed real tears each time a newly crowned Miss America slinked down the catwalk, waving to a life more promising than our own.

Time did not mellow her. As I grew older, she humiliated me more and more in front of my friends, breaking into dance at the sound of David Cassidy blaring from my record player, flirting with my friends' fathers, or the way she said "redickless" instead of "ridiculous" when shrugging off one of my mother's ideas. I cringed at her ignorance, her vanity, her childlike imprudence. In public, I walked as far away from her as I could, pretending she was not mine, feigning membership in a different family, vowing with each step to never be like her. "She can't help it," my mother had said, excusing Gracie without reason. But I didn't care. I was not going to grow up to say "redickless" or cry in front of the television and so I studied, then studied some more. I studied enough to squeak into law school and only as I packed to leave did I think I might succeed in not becoming Gracie.

Until that day I left for law school, I had believed she was my mother's sister, my aunt, Aunt Gracie, until finally my mother confessed the truth as I leaned in disbelief against the cool white tile of our kitchen counter. Gracie was not my mother's sister, but her mother. Again, Gracie's antics caught me off guard and the betrayal stung, left me shaken, uncertain, as I demanded answers to why she felt compelled to flaunt the rules of family lineage. The lie had endured for decades because Gracie had not wanted anyone to know she was old enough to have a daughter my mother's age. Years later, the lie continued unremitted as she insisted she could not be old enough to have a granddaughter. For decades she clung to her youth, turned time on its head, counterfeited herself and got away with it. Eventually the sting subsided, but from that point forward I viewed Gracie differently, both suspicious and awed by her feat.

Now an invisible roommate mumbled unintelligibly from behind a mauve curtain as I lingered beside my grandmother's bed. I surveyed Gracie's side of the room and saw eighty-five years of living reduced to fit inside two wood grain simulated bureau drawers, the surface lined with photographs of absent loved ones and good times past.

"How's school? How's your test coming?" she asked.

"Fine, fine. Everything's good."

I didn't bother to explain that school was over and had been for some time. No one in my family had attended college, let alone law school, and they had no concept of what the process involved. I offered little to further that understanding. I'd chosen to spare myself the indignity of explaining over and over how lots of people fail the bar exam the first time, not just me and no, I still wasn't a lawyer. Gracie had made it halfway through grade school and could add, but never learned to subtract. Her reading comprehension skills became suspect on an isolated family vacation at Big Bear Mountain during my junior year of high school. She, my parents and I had occupied three snowbound days in a musty rented cabin. Between games of Canasta, Monopoly and mindless TV, I read. On the second day, I peered up from my AP English copy of *Madame Bovary* to spy Gracie reclined on the couch, head resting on the overstuffed arm, reading the other book I had packed, Hunter S. Thompson's *Fear And Loathing In Las Vegas*. I kept quiet while she read for hours, plodding halfway through the book. Later, emboldened by the glass of wine cajoled from my father, I asked how she liked the story. Oblivious to Dr. Gonzo's trunk full of felonies or his ether-laced tale, she replied, "Oh, it's a good one. I love books about Las Vegas."

The volume from Gracie's roommate increased, but I still couldn't extract words from the moans. I tried to ignore it as Gracie and I attempted chit-chat. Our mutual affection for *The Guiding Light* used to prompt conversation, but bar review classes and work had eradicated that addiction on my part. Endless doctor appointments, malfunctioning televisions and nurses bent on interrupting to poke and prod had stomped out this habit for my grandmother.

Time passed.

The drone from the other side of the curtain grew louder, more persistent, until the word finally registered with a pang, "Mama...Mama...Mama."

The voice fluttered to a whimper and my brain scrambled for a quip, conversation, anything to neutralize the shock of what I just heard. But I came up empty and the woman started up again, her cries crescendoing, "Mama! Mama! MAAMAA!" The screeches slipped into screams and her voice rasped between words with what must have been phlegm, but the volume didn't let up.

The sound stabbed inside my ears and my body tensed. I knew I should do something but I didn't know what. I looked at Gracie, whose face conveyed only strained concentration.

"*MAMA! MAMA! MAMA!*"

My grandmother's head pushed back against her pillow and tilted toward the curtain. Her face contorted and I thought she was going to sneeze. Then her features twisted to a snarl, eyes flashing black. "Shut up!" she spat at the curtain, her voice sharpened into a spike. In a flicker, her face transformed back from witch, to agitated bird, then into my grandmother again. Silence fell and she turned back to me and smiled, sweet and apologetic. For a moment it was as if we were attending a garden tea party where an unladylike guest had committed a trifling faux pas. Then she closed her eyes and exhaled. For a moment she didn't seem to feel well enough to talk.

Then it started again. "MAMA! MAMA! MAMA!"

The horror of the voice's pitch made my nerve endings scream. While I knew better than to do it, I stepped past the curtain. On the mattress lay a cadaverous old woman. Matted white tufts of curls clumped her head, revealing patches of scalp and her clenched fists fought restraints that tethered her wrists to the silver bars of the bed. A blue checkered hospital gown hiked up to her chest and underneath she was naked, her shriveled legs bowed to expose a shot of her crotch. Her mouth opened wide and she howled in tempo with her head thumping against the pillow, "MAMA! MAMA!" Then her eyes rolled forward in their sockets, leveled on me and held there for a murderous look.

A shiver tickled my spine and I slid back to the other side of the curtain. Limp in her bed, my grandmother stared straight ahead at nothing.

"I'll be right back," I said.

I ventured deeper into the hallway in search of relief. I found what appeared to be a nurse's station, though only one woman sat behind the geometric arrangement of desks, her back to me. It was the same nurse from the reception desk and I caught myself looking to see if her pant seams had ripped yet.

"Excuse me," I said.

She didn't move.

"Excuse me," I said it louder that time and she turned with effort in her chair. *People* magazine rested in front of her. Under the headline, "The Woman Who Will Be Queen," Princess Diana, adorned with tiara and Armani, smiled from the cover.

"Can I help you?" An accusation, not an offering. Her eyes assessed me, adding up my youth, my possible reasons for standing there, calculating how much trouble I was capable of causing. I watched her face register the conclusion that I was not worth bothering with.

"My grandmother is in 4J and her roommate is screaming. We need to move her or—"

"I'm not her nurse."

"Isn't there someone you can call? It's terrible in there."

She sighed irritation at the interruption and twisted further around in the chair, which squeaked disapproval. She fumbled around the desk until two-inch fuchsia enameled nails clawed a laminated phone list. She consulted it with exaggerated effort.

"That's Lydia's patient. She's on break." She turned halfway back around, signaling the conversation's end.

"Listen, there must be someone who can help," my voice cracked and I paused to swallow, "No one should have to be in a room with this woman. Is there a doctor I can speak to?"

The aide snorted at my idiocy. "Girl, it's Sunday. There's no doctor here Sunday. And we don't got nobody here to be movin' patients around. She's just gonna have to wait."

I turned, my throat constricted and I knew I was about to cry. In some cultures, the elderly were revered, cherished for the wisdom collected from time and experience. In humane cultures, grandmothers were not discarded to finish their lives in rooms ringing with the shrieks of a horror film track. Poor Gracie didn't want to be a grandmother, but she was. I didn't always want to be her granddaughter, but I was. We were the same and my struggle to break away from her had been my own betrayal. Aching to be smarter, better, in control, I had shaken her influence, refused her gifts, said that what she had to bequeath me was not good enough.

As I slumped back down the hallway, I could still hear the screams and I knew I had to undo this. I would toss my flash cards, forfeit the bar exam, and get by as a law clerk at the second rate firm where I earned $12 an hour. I would care for her myself. I would scoop her up, lower her fragile bones into the torn upholstery of my front seat, drive her back to my apartment and save her. Love her.

In the Rule Against Perpetuities, the critical time is the point at which the conveyance becomes effective. An interest vests when we know someone will receive it…

Outside her room, I blinked and my mind spinned back again to a chilly Friday night in 1970. My mother had picked up a double shift at Denny's and the woman I knew as Aunt Gracie had driven me to J.C. Penny for new pajamas so I would not, in her words, "look like a ragamuffin," at the slumber party I would attend that weekend. By the time we finished, most of the stores in the mall had closed and we traversed the shadows of the deserted parking lot to her white Maverick, which looked forlorn in the lonesome darkness. She glanced behind us and paused to pull keys from her purse, then, walking again, she fumbled for a cigarette and placed it between her lips. Still yards from the car, I heard her boot smack a cement parking curb. She tumbled and fell, her body twisting before she landed with a thud on wrists and both knees. She rolled over and moaned. My eyes bulged at the sight of her torn nylons, blood seeping from her knees. I panicked. She was hurt bad. I had to go for help but I didn't know how. I saw no phone, I didn't have a dime and I didn't know who to call anyway. I was crying, then screaming. I knew I should know how to help, but I didn't.

"Jesus Christ, Tammy, stop crying," she snapped, "I'm the one that fell, not you."

She sat up, pawed inside her purse for a Kleenex and dabbed at her knees. Wiping away the blood, she had matching quarter-sized raw spots on each knee. Her hand searched the ground for the cigarette that fell, dusted off its filter tip and put it in her mouth. Her thumb clicked a green Bic lighter and I could see her crimson nails, filed into sharp points, under the flame. The cigarette had bent from the fall, but she was unaware, or didn't care, and looked like a cartoon hobo with the crooked cigarette in her mouth.

She took a long drag and exhaled a cloud of smoke, then nodded toward the car, "Come on, let's go."

Limping to the car, she slung an arm around my shoulders. "You gotta toughen up kiddo," she paused for another puff of bent cigarette, "'cause crying like that doesn't do shit."

I stood frozen in the hallway, a fuzzy perception of Gracie's gifts of moxie, nerve and fortitude seeping through. She had given me more than I realized, gifts I still needed, gifts that prepared me for any future contingency. In a world with few absolutes, the only certainty was the passage of time. For some reason we all fought that, but the Rule Against Perpetuities did not. The Rule embraced the ticking clock, embraced death even, both for their certainty. All the Rule said was that things can't stay the same forever. That seemed less difficult to grasp now.

Crossing back into 4J, tears wiped away and delusions forced down with the acid inside my stomach, I untangled the Sony Walkman from my backpack and adjusted the metal headphones while the screamer continued. Crushing one foamed circle to an ear, I rolled the radio dial in search of simple harmonious platitudes. Finding cool, clear streams of violin, I placed the sponged headphones over my grandmother's sunken skull and watched as she listened.

"Comfortable?"

She nodded as I demonstrated how to adjust the volume, tune the station. I handed her the device and her fingernails, unpainted but still shaped into points, slid the volume dial upward, then upward again. Music seeped into the room. Her eyes fluttered closed as she sank into the pillow.

"Thank you," and her cloudy eyes opened, looked at me, and meant it.

I bent down and kissed her forehead. "I have to go."

As I walked out the door I heard her whisper, "Good luck on your test."

Made in the USA
Charleston, SC
19 March 2015